Jerry Perlet's Dragon Stories 3

The Return of the Red Leprechaun

By: JERROLD PERLET

To the students of

Monocacy Elementary School

And

Sherwood Elementary School

Where the Dragon began

Author's Notes

Jerry Perlet's Dragon Stories 3: The Return of the Red Leprechaun is a continuation of the dragon adventures from **Volume 1: Sara's Adventures** and **Volume 2: George and Zoe's Adventures.** The first dragon story was told to a group of students at Monocacy Elementary School in Montgomery County, Maryland as they waited for a late bus. The setting comes from Sugarloaf Mountain and the many farm houses in the area. The adventures with the dragon were created as a part of the quarterly school assemblies. As I moved to Sherwood Elementary School, I shared the stories there as well. The children and their parents often asked where they could buy the books that I was telling the stories from. I explained that they came out of my head as I told them and there was no book.   Many families have asked to have the tales written out.

Over the years the students have asked many questions and contributed many ideas to the stories. **The Return of the Red Leprechaun** is the third volume in the series. I would like to thank the students at Broad Acres Elementary, Brooke Grove Elementary, Cedar Grove Elementary, Clearspring Elementary, Laytonsville Elementary, and Singer Elementary for contributing ideas to the stories in the third volume.

I have retired from the Montgomery County Public schools in Maryland after 38 years teaching and as an elementary principal. I have already published **Adventures with Grandpa Ek: Washington DC** and **Adventures with Grandpa Ek: Annapolis,** . Many other stories are in their beginning stages to be released in the future.

I hope you will enjoy the adventures!

Jerry Perlet

grandpaek@yahoo.com

Adventures with Grandpa Ek: Washington D.C., copyright 1978

Adventures with Grandpa Ek: Annapolis, copyright 2013

Jerry Perlet's Dragon Stories: Sara's Adventures with the Dragon, copyright 2013

Jerry Perlet's Dragon Stories2: George and Zoe's Adventures with the Dragon, copyright 2013

Jerry Perlet's Dragon Stories3: The Return of the Red Leprechaun, copyright 2014

<u>Special Thanks to:</u>

Marie Perlet, my wife and my editor.

Katie and Matthew Perlet for designing the covers.

Thanks to the **students at Broad Acres Elementary School**, Maryland, for contributing to Chapter 12.

Thanks to the **students at Brooke Grove Elementary School**, Maryland, for contributing to Chapters 4, 7, and 11.

Thanks to the **students at Cedar Grove Elementary School**, Maryland, for contributing to Chapter 10.

Thanks to the **students at Clearspring Elementary School**, Maryland, for contributing to Chapter 13.

Thanks to the **students at Laytonsville Elementary School**, Maryland, for contributing to Chapter 9.

Thanks to the **students at Singer Elementary School**, Maryland, for contributing to Chapter 8.

Table of Contents

<u>In the Middle of the Night</u>

It was the middle of the night. Someone was whispering. Zoe couldn't hear what they were saying. The hall light was on and it glowed around her bedroom door. Zoe looked at her clock, it was 2:04. What was going on?

Zoe slipped out of bed and opened the bedroom door. Her dad was standing at the top of the stairs holding a small suitcase. He came over to her.

"Daddy, is everything okay?"

"Everything is fine, honey. It's time for the babies to come and so we are going to the hospital. Uncle Matt and Aunt Katie will be here in about five minutes and then we are leaving. I'll call you from the hospital to let you know when the babies arrive."

"Is Mommy okay?"

"She is great, Zoe. She is just ready to have these babies."

"Tell her we love her and we'll see her at the hospital."

"I will tell her. You climb back into bed and get some sleep. Matt and Katie will be here, so you and George take good care of them. Good night, sweetie."

Zoe closed the door and shuffled across the room, half asleep. She looked out the window at the mountain. There was a glowing orange light way up near the top. She grabbed her binoculars and stared at the light. It was the entrance to the dragon's cave. They had never found the outside entrance even though George and Zoe had searched the mountaintop over and over. Then she saw the dragon's shadow fly across the orange light and up into the sky. Where was he going at this hour?

She would be sure to ask him the next time she saw him. Zoe shuffled past George's bed and snuggled back under her covers. Whatever was going on at the hospital she was sure it would be fine. She would find out about it all in the morning.

It was a beautiful Thursday morning in late April. George and Zoe jumped out of bed and ran to the window. The sky was blue, the sun was bright, and the mountain was beginning to have that spring glow of newborn green leaves. Luckily for them it was their spring vacation and there wasn't any school this week.

"George, Mom and Dad went to the hospital last night. It was time for the babies to come."

"What? You didn't wake me up?" George poked Zoe in the ribs.

She gave him a gentle shove back and said, "Why would you get up to just say goodbye and go back to bed. Anyways, you were sleeping so soundly, I don't think you would have heard a word I said.

"And when I went back to bed, I saw the dragon fly out of his cave on the top of the mountain. What do you think he was doing up at that hour?"

"Maybe he heard the voices in the hallway, too," George grinned at Zoe.

"All right, that's enough. Uncle Matt and Aunt Katie are supposed to be here to look after us until Daddy gets back. Let's go check."

The children got dressed and headed down the hallway to the stairs. As they passed the guest room, they could hear loud snoring coming from the bedroom. They looked in and Uncle Matt and Aunt Katie were passed out on the bed still in their clothes.

"When do you think they will wake up?" George whispered.

"I don't know. We can go down and make breakfast and then surprise them."

"What do you think they eat for breakfast?"

A voice answered from the bed, "Eggs. Bacon. And coffee."

Another voice said, "Lots of bacon and strong coffee."

Zoe and George looked at each other and smiled. Matt and Katie were awake. They ran to the bed and jumped on top of their uncle. He rolled over and threw Zoe onto the pillows and then held George in the air above him. Katie rolled over to make room for the little ones.

"All right, you mateys, it's time for a big country breakfast with all the fixin's."

George laughed as his uncle swung him down onto the bed. "What are fixin's?"

"Them thar is the good things that you put around the food on the plate, like the syrup and the cheese and the chocolate and the powdered sugar. All the good stuff!" The kids loved it when Uncle Matt talked like a pirate.

"So, Captain Matt, do pirates know how to cook?"

"Oh no, Ms. Zoe. But they bring along their wenches to cook for them, and they kidnap little children to do all the cleaning. So, you mateys should take wench Katie down to the galley and cook me up my breakfast! Arrrgh!"

Uncle Matt stood up and stretched. Katie groaned and rolled out of bed. "Captain Pirate needs to make his own breakfast so the wench can sleep!" Everyone chuckled and George and Zoe gave Aunt Katie a big hug. George smiled at her and said, "Come on wench, we'll make breakfast together."

Then George and Zoe jumped on Matt's back and he carried them down the stairs to the kitchen. Katie set about finding the food and utensils to make breakfast and they all cooked up quite a feast.

"Have you heard from Daddy?"

"Nope, nothing yet. Let me look at my phone messages." Uncle Matt took out his cell phone. He pushed some buttons and looked at his messages.

"It says here that they made it to the hospital just fine. The doctors think the babies will be born at sunrise. Your dad will call when they are delivered. So we should be hearing something soon because I definitely see the sun is rising over the mountain."

As if by magic, the phone rang and Matt answered, "Hello?"

"Zoe and George are great. We're having breakfast. How are you two? I'll put you on speaker phone." Uncle Matt pushed a button and the children could hear their dad.

"Hey, everybody! Your new little brother and sister have arrived. They are each about 5 pounds which is good for twins. Your mom is resting now. I'm going to hang around here for a while to make sure all is well and then I will head home by ten o'clock. The doctors said that you can visit this afternoon."

"All right!" George let out a big whoop.

"Also, your mom said to tell you that you don't need to go to the cave today. He is not there. I guess you know what that is about. Didn't make any sense to me, but I promised to give you that message."

Zoe looked at George with questioning eyes. George shrugged his shoulders in reply. Uncle Matt and Aunt Katie just shook their heads. "I suppose she's talking about that dragon again. Sometimes I think all that health food my sister eats makes her think weird thoughts."

"Anyways, I'll see you all later this morning. Thanks for coming over, Matt and Katie. We really appreciate your help. I'll call Tom and Emily and let them know about the twins. You kids take good care of your aunt and uncle."

"Don't worry, we will," George said with a bit of a sly twist.

"Bye, Daddy. See you later." Uncle Matt ended the call.

"So, what do you do after you eat your breakfast?" Katie asked.

"Oh, we watch TV all morning, at least two or three hours of cartoons. And we eat lots of candy, too."

"George, you shouldn't tell your aunt fibs. We each get to watch one half hour of cartoons and then we have to go outside and play. We don't get any candy until the afternoon." Zoe smiled at George.

"All right, I get to watch my pirate show and then you can watch your show about the fairies in the woods. Like they really exist or something."

The children helped their aunt and uncle clean up breakfast and then they settled down in front of the TV. Katie and Matt took a nap on the sofa and they all waited anxiously for their dad to return.

The New Twins

Around 10 a.m. George and Zoe's father came home from the hospital. He showed everyone the pictures of their new twin brother and sister. Dad said that their mom was doing well and wanted them to visit this afternoon. Zoe and George couldn't wait. Jim thanked Katie and Matt for taking care of George and Zoe. Matt said that Uncle Tom had called and he and Aunt Emily would be coming over tomorrow to see the babies and help out. He also said that all the grandparents had called and were planning to arrive sometime on Saturday. It seemed like the whole family was coming to visit. Uncle Matt and Aunt Katie gave Zoe and George big hugs and told their dad how well they behaved and then they headed home.

"We have a lot to do to get ready for all this company. Let's get busy." Dad told Zoe and George what chores they needed to get done before they could go to the hospital. The children got busy and completed everything by noon. Then they settled down to a big lunch. Zoe decided to make a card welcoming the new babies. George wanted to help, so they worked together to make a big picture of the whole family and Zoe wrote across the top, 'Welcome to the family!' They both signed the card and George put it by the front door to take to the hospital.

At 3 p.m. Dad announced it was time to go. They climbed into the van and Zoe noticed that there were two more car seats. George started to complain about having to sit in the far back seat and Zoe put her hand on his shoulder. "It's not that bad, George, and you always said you wanted to sit back here with me. To tell you the truth, Mom and Dad can't see me sneaking candy back here, so just be quiet and enjoy the ride." George took the piece of candy that Zoe handed him and he was quiet. After a while he told his dad how much he enjoyed the back seat. Zoe and George giggled quietly.

As they drove down the road, Dad explained that their mom would be pretty tired and her tummy would hurt for a while, so they needed to be careful about jumping on her or hugging her too hard. George and Zoe loved to wrestle with their mom and dad, so it was important for them to understand their mom's current condition. He assured them that she would be much better within a few days.

"Dad, are these babies going to cry all the time?"

"Not all the time, George. But right now that is the only way they can let us know that they are hungry, want their diapers changed, or just need a hug. You'll learn how to tell the difference in their cries."

"Well, as long as I don't have to change those stinky diapers."

"Oh George, I'm sure your mother and I will handle that."

"When will the babies be able to call us by our names?"

"That will take a while, George. You started saying mama and dada when you were about six months old. So don't expect them to call you anything other than 'Whaaaa' for a while."

They arrived at the hospital and parked the car. Zoe and George skipped along the sidewalk to the front door and waited for their dad. He joined them and showed them how he had to check in each time he visited. Then they went up in the elevator and into the Maternity Ward. There were a lot of crying babies and nurses everywhere.

Zoe wondered if her mom got any sleep with all this noise. Her dad assured her that her mom's room was soundproof so she didn't hear all the crying.

The children entered room fifteen and saw their mom in bed resting. She opened her eyes and smiled at them. "Oh, it is so great to see you two! Thanks for coming to visit. How are Katie and Matt doing?"

The two children told their mom everything about the morning in rapid fire. Then George asked, "Where are the babies?"

"They are resting in the nursery right now. The nurses will bring them soon for their next feeding."

Zoe turned to look out the window and saw the dragon sitting in a chair taking a nap. She went over and gently tapped on the dragon's shoulder. She whispered, "Good morning, Mr. Dragon. What are you doing here?"

The dragon opened an eye and said, "Good morning, Zoe. I always come to your family deliveries to watch over the mother and the babies. I was here when you were born and also when George arrived. In fact, I was here when your grandmother was born as well as your mother. It is part of my job to look after all of you.

"It looks like everything is fine here, so I am going to head back to my cave to get some rest. It was a long night. I'll see you at the cave in the next few days."

"Thanks for looking after my mom and the babies, Mr. Dragon. We'll see you soon."

As the dragon quietly tiptoed over to the doorway, Sara said, "Thanks" and winked. The dragon waved and moved down the hallway. He squeezed into the elevator and George and Zoe laughed as he pulled his tail into the elevator before the doors closed.

A nurse brought the twins to room fifteen and Zoe and George went back to their mother's room to see the new babies.

"So, what are we going to call them? How about Thing 1 and Thing 2?"

"Oh, George, that is so silly! Dr. Seuss used those names and they are not appropriate for babies!"

"What do you want to call them, Zoe? Barbie and Ken?"

"Very funny, George. No wonder Mom and Dad didn't ask you for any names."

Sara calmed the children by putting her hands on their heads. "Listen you two. We all have a lot of work to do in the next few months taking care of these newborns. I need you to help and not argue all the time."

George groaned, "Okay, as long as I don't have to change those dirty diapers."

Zoe sighed, "All right, George. You don't have to change the diapers, but you will need to help feed them. You can hold a bottle and talk nicely to them. You can do that, can't you?"

"Yeah, I can do that! That sounds like fun."

Sara held Jim's hand and announced the babies' names. "We are going to call the girl Annabel and the boy will be Nathan. Annie and Nate will be their nicknames."

"Welcome to our family, Annie and Nate," Zoe said as she patted Annie's head. George stroked Nate's cheek and said, "We guys are going to stick together and watch out for the girls."

Everyone laughed and then Jim took Zoe and George home to rest. Sara and the babies would stay in the hospital overnight and come home tomorrow. There was a lot to do at home to get ready.

A Morning Hike

Aunt Emily and Uncle Tom arrived around dinnertime. George and Zoe raced to greet them and tell them all about the babies. Emily and Tom helped the family get everything ready for the babies while Jim cooked up his famous barbeque chicken. After dinner they all went for a walk along the lane towards the mountain. Then it was time for bed.

George and Zoe asked Tom to read them bedtime stories. They snuggled together on George's bed and Tom read the next chapter in the Ramona Quimby book they had been reading. Then he pulled out his favorite, "Mike Mulligan and his Steam Shovel", and George and Zoe smiled. Even though that was a book for little kids, they always loved to hear Uncle Tom read it. He added so many voices and funny things to the story.

Aunt Emily and Dad came in to join them and they all looked out the window together at the stars. Emily said, "You sure have a beautiful view of the mountain. It must be fun to wake up each morning and see how it has changed. Do you guys go up there much?"

Zoe responded, "We love the mountain. Every day it has something new to teach us. And best of all, our dragon lives up there."

"Oh yes, I've heard about the famous dragon. Your mom tells me about him all the time. Your uncles need to remember more about their childhood adventures up there, right Tom?" Emily poked Tom in the shoulder and he shook his head. He could sense something about the mountain but he couldn't remember all that had happened there. There couldn't really be dragons, so it all seemed kind of silly. But maybe he would take a hike up there tomorrow just for old time's sake.

Everyone went to bed eagerly awaiting the arrival of Nate and Annie.

* * * *

The next morning George and Zoe awoke to a terrible thunderstorm. Lightning was flashing everywhere on the mountain and the rain was coming down in buckets. "This certainly isn't a good way to welcome Annie and Nate to our house," George said.

They got dressed and raced down to the kitchen for breakfast. Aunt Emily was cooking up one of her famous omelets and George and Zoe eagerly slid into their chairs with their forks ready. There was a big pile of freshly-baked blueberry muffins, bowls of blueberries, strawberries, and orange slices, and big glasses of orange juice to wash it all down. This was a scrumptious breakfast.

Dad and Tom joined the group and they all enjoyed the feast. Dad explained the events for the day. "I'll go to the hospital this morning to get your mom and the babies. You two stay here with Tom and Emily. We will leave the hospital around noon and we should get here by 1 p.m. I'll call when we get on the road so that you will be ready for our arrival."

"Sounds good to me. How about a hike up the mountain this morning to get some exercise?" Uncle Tom was full of surprises and George, Zoe, and Emily all agreed that a hike would be fun.

"Except, what about the rain?"

"I think it is going to stop soon and I am sure you two are good in the mud!" Everyone laughed.

Jim waved goodbye and left in the van to get Sara and the twins. Zoe and George put on their hiking boots and joined Tom and Emily at the back door ready to climb the mountain trail. "Uncle Matt and I used to climb this trail all the time. We loved to reach the top and see the world below us."

"I heard that my mom usually led the way."

"Only when we let her."

"Like the night you found the dragon?"

"Ha, there you go again with those dragon stories, Zoe."

They climbed the slippery trail towards a large boulder. The rain had stopped and the sun was beginning to break through the clouds. George hummed a tune, "The Bear Went Over the Mountain", and they all joined in to sing a chorus. As they reached the boulder, George stopped. He put his finger to his lips and whispered to everyone to be quiet.

Tom whispered back, "What's the matter? You think you are going to find a dragon on the other side?" Then he started laughing out loud.

Emily poked Tom in the ribs and marched around the rock ahead of Tom and the children. She stopped with a start and backed up. "This isn't possible. What on earth?"

Zoe and George rushed past Emily to see what surprised her. They remembered all too well the first time they had gone around this boulder and found the dragon in the rain and mud very sick from poison berries. Surely their Aunt Emily couldn't see the dragon.

As they rounded the boulder they were astonished to find the dragon sitting on a patch of grass in the clearing, staring at the sky. He seemed to be mesmerized by the clouds and he did not look at all right to the children. Of course, Emily was amazed to see a dragon, but Zoe and George were very concerned that he did not appear to be okay.

George and Zoe ran to the dragon. "Mr. Dragon, are you all right?" Zoe asked.

The dragon did not respond. He continued to stare into the sky. The children climbed up onto his back as Emily and Tom just stood and stared at the dragon.

"Tom? I'm not sure that I am seeing this. Do you see it, too? Is this the dragon from your childhood?"

"I see him, Emily, but I can't explain it. He always said that adults couldn't see him because we didn't believe.

I guess it is all right for Zoe and George to climb on him like that?"

"They seem to know him very well. Let's see what happens."

Zoe climbed all the way up to the dragon's nose and stared into his eyes. She waved her hands in his face and yelled as loudly as she could, "Don't you see me, Mr. Dragon? I'm right here. Wake up!"

George grabbed the dragon's tail and tried to swing it back and forth. It was much too heavy, and the dragon seemed to be in a trance and did not help. He climbed up the dragon's back to his ears. He tried to wiggle the ears, but the dragon did not respond. He just continued to stare into the sky. Zoe and George looked up where the dragon was staring to see if they could figure out what he was staring at. They both saw it at the same time and Zoe yelled to George, "Look away!"

She slid across the dragon's head and pushed George so that his gaze was broken and they both fell to the ground. Emily and Tom rushed over.

"What is the matter? Is the dragon okay? What's wrong?"

"The dragon is staring at a bright red light up in the clouds. Somehow it is hypnotizing him. We have to figure out a way to block the light to get him out of this trance. I am really worried about this light. This is not normal."

George asked Emily for the backpack. Emily pulled it off and Tom grabbed the blanket they had brought along for their picnic. He handed it to George. "Here, try this."

George yelled to Zoe, "I've got this. We can use it to cover his eyes."

The children climbed up the dragon's back and they went on either side of his ears. George threw one end of the blanket to Zoe and they covered the dragon's eyes. Zoe quickly tied a knot to keep the blindfold on the dragon, which was a good thing because the dragon let out a terrible roar and shook his head. Zoe and George fell off into the bushes.

"What have you done with the beautiful red light?" the dragon roared. "I love the red light. Where has it gone?" He swung his giant head back and forth, but the blindfold held. Gradually the dragon calmed down and he seemed to be coming out of the trance. He shook his head several times and tried to claw off the blanket. Thank goodness Zoe had tied tight knots.

Finally the dragon spoke in his normal voice. "Children? Are you there? I am okay now. Thank you for saving me. You can take the blindfold off."

"Are you sure, Mr. Dragon? We don't want you to look at the light again. Are you going to look up again?"

"No, now I know what it is and I will be sure to look away."

George climbed up and loosened the blanket. As it fell away, the dragon smiled and looked down at the children and Emily and Tom. "I see you have brought me some company. How good to see you again, Tom. And welcome to the mountain, Emily. It is a pleasure to meet you."

Tom and Emily said hello and they all sat down on the ground on the blanket. George got water for everyone and some peanut butter sandwiches. "So, Mr. Dragon, what was that all about? What is that red light?"

Tom and Emily just kept staring at the dragon, more than twenty feet long and glowing a beautiful green color. His eyes were kind and they could tell he was a good dragon. Tom tried so hard to remember the dragon from his childhood. As the dragon spoke he could remember a few moments of their adventures.

"This has happened to me once before and your uncles saved me. We were playing a game of soccer in this same clearing and there was a ringing sound up in the sky. I looked up and saw this beautiful red light and I couldn't stop looking at it."

Tom continued the story, "Yeah, and you went into that trance and we couldn't get you to stop staring at the light. I finally kicked the soccer ball at your head and it knocked you down and then you stopped staring at the sky. You said something about the red leprechaun. And then we just went on playing soccer and forgot about it."

Zoe and George turned to the dragon. "It can't be the red leprechaun. You banished him in a locked stone box to Ireland. He can't come back. And how can the adults see you? I thought only children could see you. What is going on, Mr. Dragon?"

"You remember that your mother can see me because she really wants to believe. Your Aunt Emily really wants to believe, so she can see me. Your Uncle Tom is remembering his past so he can see me, too."

"So will Uncle Matt, Aunt Katie, and my dad be able to see you?"

"I really don't know. It depends on whether they want to. I am not sure if the red light is the red leprechaun. I will contact Pedraic the dragon in Ireland to find out if the leprechaun has escaped."

Tom looked at his watch. "We need to get going, children. The babies will be home soon. Good to see you again, Mr. Dragon. I hope we will meet again soon."

"I am so impressed with your green scales and your friendly eyes, Mr. Dragon. Thank you for letting me see you," Emily said.

Zoe turned to the dragon and asked, "Will you be okay now? No more looking at red lights."

George added, "And we need to know if the red leprechaun has escaped. He is very dangerous."

"We will meet again soon, children. I will find out about the red leprechaun and I won't be looking at any red lights. Hurry home to welcome Annie and Nate."

The group moved down the path as they waved goodbye to the dragon. Emily kept looking over her shoulder to check one more time for the dragon. She was really impressed.

Tom's phone rang as they reached the house. "Okay Jim, we'll see you soon. We have lunch ready and we'll come out to help carry everything into the house."

Sara, Jim, and the babies arrived around one o'clock. Tom and Emily each took one of the babies and Jim helped Sara into the house. George and Zoe carried all the baby bags and supplies from the hospital. "They sure gave Mom a lot of stuff there. I guess she knows what to do with all of it."

They went into the house and settled in the family room. George and Zoe showed their card to the babies even though they were fast asleep. Sara thanked them for the beautiful card. Tom and Emily served everyone lunch while they watched the babies sleep. All was good in Zoe and George's world.

<u>The Great Wall of China</u>

It was the Saturday morning after Annie and Nate had arrived home. Zoe and George awoke to a beautiful sunny day and the air smelled so sweet. It was so good to have spring back. The winter had been long and cold and the children were looking forward to the warmer weather so they could play outside more often. They got dressed and dashed down to breakfast.

Sara was up making some scrambled eggs and sausage. The coffee was brewing and breakfast smells filled the air. Tom and Emily stumbled into breakfast. "Coffee....I need coffee," Tom said. "Long night, huh, sis?"

"Oh, not too bad for a first night. The babies will adjust to their new surroundings. Thanks for helping out so much during the night. I guess all the grandparents will be arriving today."

"I'll call Matt and Katie and invite them. We can have an informal family barbeque this afternoon and Matt can do the grilling."

Sara responded, "I think that would be great. I could use all the help I can get right now, so why not feed everyone and enjoy our newest family members."

Tom called Matt and then the grandparents. Everyone planned to bring something and have a big picnic dinner. George and Zoe asked if they could be excused for the morning. Sara gave them a knowing look and said, "Yes, I think he is expecting you. It is okay to invite him to the picnic, too. Say hi for me and thank him again for being there."

Aunt Emily added, "And tell him that I enjoyed meeting him and I hope to see him again soon." Sara looked surprised and while Zoe and George raced out the door, Emily told her about their hike up the mountain.

The children reached the large oak tree and knocked three times. The magic door opened and they climbed inside the tree. They descended the spiral staircase to the yellow path and ran all the way to the dragon's cave doorway. They knocked on the door frame.

"Good morning, children. Come on in. How are things at your house? Did the babies keep you up last night?"

"It's only been one night, Mr. Dragon. I am sure they will stop crying all the time by tonight."

"Well, George, sorry to tell you that the babies will cry for some time, maybe even for a year."

"What? How am I ever going to get any sleep?"

"Oh, don't be silly, George. You snored all night so I am sure that you got a lot of sleep, unlike me who not only had to listen to babies, but you too!" They giggled as they settled on the couch with the dragon.

"Mr. Dragon, Mom told me to invite you to the family picnic this afternoon. My grandparents and my aunts and uncles are coming. I am sure there will be lots to eat."

"Thank you, Zoe. I will plan on attending."

"And Aunt Emily says hi, too. I think she likes you, Mr. Dragon," George said with a smile. "Why can all these adults see you?"

"That is an interesting question, George. This has never happened before. First your grandmother and then your mother. Now your aunts and uncles. I am thinking that we need to make a quick trip to the Grand Master in China to find out why this is happening. I am also curious about the red light in the sky. I have not heard back from Pedraic in Ireland. The Master may know something about that, too."

"China! Oh boy! That sounds like fun. When do we go?"

"It shouldn't take long. We can go now and be back for the picnic this afternoon."

Zoe and George put sandwiches and bottles of water into their backpacks and climbed aboard the dragon's back. They flew out of the cave and up into the clouds heading for China. Because the dragon is magical, they arrived in China in a flash and landed on a large wall.

"Whoa, this wall goes on for miles and miles. Who built this?"

"This is the Great Wall of China, Zoe. The wall has existed for thousands of years. It is estimated to be over 5,500 miles long. It was built to protect China from invaders and to control trade with foreign countries. Over the centuries they have added watch towers and forts. People could also travel over the top of the wall for miles. It is an amazing feat of construction. Parts of the wall are actually trenches and natural features that block invasion.

"We are here because the Grand Dragon Master lives within the wall. We will find him at the fifth tower from here, so let's begin our walk."

"But can't we just fly there?" asked George.

"We must show respect for the Dragon Master and so we must approach his tower on foot. That is the tradition, George."

The three walked along the wall for some time passing each tower. As they approached the fifth tower, the dragon stood tall and bellowed out a loud roar. A larger dragon rose out of the top of the tower and roared in response, "Come Edward, the path is open to you and your friends."

"Edward? Who is that?" Zoe wanted to know.

"That is my real name, Zoe. Everyone always calls me Mr. Dragon, but there are so many dragons in China we must have names. I am Edward the Dragon."

The three crossed the wall and entered the tower. They descended a very long stairway down into the underground. When they reached the bottom, they found a large pond of water. There was no bridge. On the far side they could see a tunnel lit by torches.

"I will cross the water and enter the Grand Master's cave. You will wait here for my return."

"Mr. Dragon, don't you see the alligators in the water? How are you going to cross without getting bitten?"

"There are ways to cross water infested with alligators. Watch as I go."

The dragon first dipped his toe into the water. All the alligators came to the surface eager for a bite of the visitor. The dragon then jumped on top of each alligator's head using them as stepping stones across the water. He was so quick that the alligators did not have time to bite him. When he reached the far bank, he jumped towards the ground. One sly alligator had waited right near the shore and as the dragon jumped, he bit the dragon's tail. The dragon fell onto the ground and let out a terrible roar of pain. "You are always the wise one, waiting until the end. That hurt, but I will mend."

The alligator smiled at the dragon and then sank into the water. The children looked across the water to be sure the dragon was safe. "Are you okay?"

"Yes, children, I am fine. Just a little nip that will soon heal. I will meet with the Grand Master and return shortly."

The children settled down on a rock and ate their sandwiches while they waited. The alligators kept swimming around looking at the children. "George, I don't like those gators looking at us."

"Well, Zoe, I don't think they can come out of the water and they probably just like the look of your great sandwiches." As the children finished their lunch, the alligators lost interest and floated away.

After an hour or so, the dragon came back out of the tunnel. He dipped his claw in the water again, the alligators all came to the surface, and he jumped across again. This time he avoided the old sly gator and landed safely on the ground near Zoe and George.

"What did he say?"

"The Grand Master knew about the red light and said the leprechaun has escaped. They cannot find Pedraic either. He is not sure why the adults can see me, perhaps because they are all related to you. But I think I need to get out of here and find some medicine for my tail. It is swelling up and it really hurts. This has never happened before when the alligator bit me. There must be something in the water that infected my tail."

The group climbed the stairway and went outside on the wall. There were several people walking along the wall and they stopped and marveled at the dragon, many waving and smiling. Apparently, dragons were a usual thing around here.

Zoe asked them, "Does anyone know where we can find some medicine for the dragon's tail? He has a nasty bite from an alligator."

Many shook their heads no, but one little girl about Zoe's age stepped forward. "We use the magic mud from the river bank to cure alligator bites. If you look over the wall down there, you will see that most of the mud is brown, but there is a patch of red mud right there." She pointed. "You can use the stairs over there and get down to the riverbank. Take this bucket. Watch out for the alligators in the river. They will attack you if you are not careful."

The dragon was now lying down on top of the wall. "It seems this bite is worse than I thought. I am feeling so sleepy."

George and Zoe dashed down the stairs to the riverbank. While George scooped up a whole bucket full of red mud, Zoe watched the river for alligators. "There are two of them coming our way. Are you finished?"

"Got it! Let's go."

The children climbed the riverbank and then the stairs back to the top of the wall. The dragon was now fast asleep on the wall and his color was beginning to fade to blue. Zoe knew this was not a good sign. George took the mud from the bucket and spread it all over the dragon's tail and especially into the bite. Everyone watched anxiously to see what would happen.

The dragon did not move and his breathing was slowing down. "It's not working. What else can we try?"

The girl stepped to the dragon's side and said, "You must be patient. Concentrate on the dragon's bite. Tell it to heal. Tell the dragon to get better."

George looked at Zoe for some guidance. She shrugged her shoulders and said, "Let's do it, George. Stare at the bite and tell Mr. Dragon to get better." Zoe and George stared and chanted and suddenly the dragon began to turn green again. Then he groaned and sat up. He stretched out his arms and wings and let out a loud groan. Everyone stepped back.

"You have done a good deed today, children. You saved my life."

"Thanks, Mr. Dragon, but this little girl is the hero. She knew about the red mud and she told us we had to be patient and concentrate. She saved you."

The dragon turned to the little girl. "You have done a very brave thing today. Your family will be blessed for generations to come. Thank you."

The little girl bowed her head. "It is an honor to save a dragon, especially one who is such a beautiful green color. Thank you for your blessing. I will share it with my family." Zoe hugged the little girl and thanked her over and over. Then the girl continued her walk along the top of the wall towards her home.

"Children, it is time for us to go. We don't want to be late for the barbeque." They climbed aboard the dragon's back and waved goodbye to all the people on the wall. The dragon flew into the clouds and soon the children saw their house and the family gathering for the barbeque. The dragon flew down to the backyard and landed near the big oak tree.

"You go along and see your family. I will come soon. I need to rest a little bit and get cleaned up." The dragon rose into the sky and flew back to his cave, and Zoe and George joined their parents, their aunts and uncles, their grandparents, and the new twins for the big party. The dragon came back a short time later and joined the party. The food was delicious and everyone had a great time celebrating the arrival of Nate and Annie.

* * * * * * * * * * * * * * * *

After the dinner party the grandparents left, and Emily and Katie helped Sara clean up. Zoe and George settled down on the couch with their dad to read some books. Matt and Tom decided to go for a walk on the trail towards the mountain.

"Did you see the dragon at dinner?" Tom asked.

Matt looked at Tom with a frown. "Did you really see a dragon at dinner?"

"Emily and I both saw him. You know Sara can see him. I am really surprised that you can't."

"To tell you the truth, from time to time I think I see him, usually his tail going around a corner. Sometimes I feel his warm breath over my shoulder. And I dream about him once in a while. I did see him at dinner, but since adults aren't supposed to see him, I didn't want people to think I was crazy."

"Something is up because almost everyone in the family can see him now. Does Katie see him?"

"She has not mentioned it, but I think I will tell her that I can and hear what she says. Why do you think we are all seeing him now?"

There was a rustling sound in the bushes and then the dragon stepped out onto the trail. "Hello, Matt and Tom. We need to talk." The three sat down on a big rock, just like old times. "The Grand Master in China has explained all this to me. Soon there will be a magical problem that we will need all the adults and children to help solve. You will need to understand the problem and the solution and share it with Sara. If Jim, Emily, and Katie are willing to help, that will add energy to the fight."

The three walked along the path for another half an hour as the dragon explained all that the Grand Master had revealed. Matt and Tom thanked the dragon and they returned to the house. Zoe and George were in bed and the adults were in the living room relaxing and admiring the twins. Matt and Tom came in and said they needed to have a family meeting to discuss a serious matter from the dragon. The adults gathered in a circle and heard all that the Grand Master had revealed.

The Lake Vacation

It was summer, their favorite time of the year. George and Zoe jumped out of bed and ran to the window. It was a beautiful day with bright sunshine and cool breezes. "Zoe, today is the day we go to Uncle Tom's house for a week!"

"I'm all packed. Did you get everything into your suitcase?"

"Everything except my toys. I put them in a separate bag."

"George, sometimes I think you have too many toys. We're going to play in the lake and the woods and do all those summery things. You won't have time for toys."

"And I suppose you packed some books to read and your dolls. When will you have time to play with that stuff?"

Zoe poked George in the ribs. "All right, we both have our things we want to take. I only took one of my stuffed animals, but I do have about ten books I want to read. If it is like last summer, I won't even get one read. Emily and Tom have so many fun things for us to do."

The children got dressed and raced down to breakfast. Sara had made their favorites---big fluffy pancakes with lots of gooey syrup and large glasses of orange juice. They gobbled it all down.

"We're ready to go, Mom. Do you think the dragon will come visit us at Tom and Emily's?"

"You never know with the dragon. He likes to keep an eye on you two." But Sara did know that the dragon was keeping a constant vigil protecting her children from the red light. Zoe and George did not know anything about it and she wanted to keep it that way. No need to worry them on their summer vacation.

Jim brought down the suitcases and backpacks and everyone piled into the van. George and Zoe got the back seat, Annie and Nate were in the middle, and Mom and Dad were in the front. Off they went to Tom and Emily's house on the lake.

Emily and Tom had built a beautiful house on a lake nearby. They had a swimming dock, kayaks, a motor boat, and a row boat. There was a little island in the middle of the lake and George and Zoe always loved to paddle over to the island pretending they were pirates hiding their treasures. Emily would hide costume jewelry and plastic gold coins around the yard and in the house, and the children would find the treasure and load it into a small wooden chest. Then they would row across the lake and bury it somewhere on the island. Tom always had a map for them to fill out so they could find the treasure the next day.

During the week they would hike around the lake, have campfires at night and roast marshmallows. George loved S'mores and Zoe knew how to cook hot dogs on sticks. The lake was always a favorite place to visit and their aunt and uncle made it so special.

One night they decided to sleep outside in a tent. While George and Zoe tried to settle down inside the tent, Tom and Emily took turns watching from the porch to be sure that some creature did not visit during the night. About every two hours they would relieve each other for a quick nap. The children finally passed out around 1 a.m. and Tom and Emily enjoyed a cup of tea on the porch and watched the moon rise over the lake while the stars were twinkling above. There was a refreshing breeze that came from the nearby pine forest. It was so peaceful here.

And then the red light came out of nowhere. It was drifting over the treetops and headed for the house and the tent. It moved slowly back and forth as if it were searching for something. Tom and Emily knew exactly what to do since the dragon had warned them that this could happen anytime. They grabbed their sunglasses, their very bright flashlights, and mirrors, and they moved quickly to the tent. They turned off their lights and sat quietly in front of the tent watching the dark sky. They put on their sunglasses. The red light floated closer and finally began to move towards the tent.

Tom could see that the light was really a large bubble with a red leprechaun inside. He was a very ugly little man. This was the evil red leprechaun who had tried to steal the dragons' gold and Zoe and George had saved the dragons' treasures by tricking the leprechaun. His name was Logan and he was supposed to be locked in a stone box with a magic lock and banished to Ireland forever. He had escaped somehow and was now trying to kidnap Zoe and George. The leprechaun was wearing a red suit and hat and had an evil smile. When he saw Emily and Tom, he started cackling his creepy laugh.

"You would be wise to be gone or you will suffer a terrible fate. Move!"

Emily and Tom stood their ground and stared at the leprechaun. Emily yelled, "You would be wiser to get out of here right now before we lock you back in that stone box!"

The leprechaun howled at this threat. "The box comes from the dragons, not you foolish humans. Prepare yourselves for terrible pain!"

The leprechaun pointed his fingers at Tom and Emily and giant flashes of lightning shot at them. Tom and Emily raised their mirrors and reflected the bolts back at the leprechaun. The lightning burst the bubble and the leprechaun fell to the ground. They shined their powerful flashlights on him and he groaned. "I'll be back!" And with that he disappeared in a flash of fire and smoke.

George and Zoe came to the tent entrance. "What was that all about?"

Emily grabbed George's hand and Tom picked up Zoe. "Come along, children. The camping trip is over and we have much to tell you."

They ran into the house and closed all the drapes. Tom called Sara while Emily settled the children on the sofa and began to explain what was happening. Sara told Tom to bring the children home immediately. She would try to summon the dragon for help.

Emily explained that all the adults met after the barbeque and Matt and Tom told them what the dragon had learned from the Grand Master. He explained that the red leprechaun had escaped from the stone box and was hunting for the dragons' gold. The leprechaun planned to kidnap Zoe and George and use them for ransom to get the gold. Everyone had to be ready to protect the children if the red light showed up.

The Grand Master had given the dragon directions on how to protect people from the leprechaun. They needed to wear sunglasses, have bright lights, and large mirrors. They could reflect the lightning bolts back at the leprechaun and shine the strong lights on him. He could not bear the strong beams. The sunglasses would protect the adults from the mesmerizing red light.

Tom and Emily had been prepared and did exactly what the dragon said. "Thank goodness it worked. He was a nasty little man. Your mother wants us to get you home now. She is trying to contact the dragon for help. Let's pack up and move out."

Within ten minutes the four were in the car speeding down the road towards the children's home. George and Zoe were not worried, but they were angry that their week at the lake had been cut short by this red elf. They stared out the window watching for a red light. The mountain loomed in the darkness and George could just make out an orange glowing spot near the top. He announced, "The dragon is up."

<u>The River Vacation</u>

It was a warm and sunny morning in early August. The children awoke to singing birds and a fresh breeze through their window. No one had seen the red light since the July night at Emily and Tom's. The dragon had put a protection spell around the children's property so they were safe to play in their yard and at the dragon's cave. They had been on several adventures with the dragon this summer and everything seemed normal. Today they were going to Uncle Matt and Aunt Katie's house for their summer week at the river.

George and Zoe bounded out of bed and got dressed in a hurry. Their suitcases and backpacks were already

packed. They raced down to a breakfast of pancakes, gooey syrup, and orange juice. Sara had prepared a bowl of blueberries as well. Their mom made the best breakfasts.

Then all six of them piled into the van and headed for Matt and Katie's. The twins were now about three months old and they were cooing and smiling. George had fun making them laugh. Zoe was the big sister, feeding them and giving them a bath once in a while. The family sang songs as they drove down to the river road.

Zoe knew they were almost there when they passed a big old red barn. They turned right onto a dirt road and went down to Uncle Matt's river house. It was a very modern deck house built on stilts into the hillside along the river. When the river flooded, the house was safely above the waters. There were large windows that looked out on the river valley and you could see for miles. George felt like a bird up in the trees when they stayed at this house.

The children jumped out of the car and raced across the deck to the front door. Aunt Katie met them with a big hug and a plate of her famous chocolate chip cookies. Their parents came along with the twins while Uncle Matt grabbed the suitcases and backpacks.

"Things have been quiet these past few weeks?"

Sara replied, "Yes, Matt. The dragon put a protection spell around our property. But I have to admit that I am a little worried about them staying here without that protection. The dragon actually cornered that leprechaun up on the top of the mountain, but he used his red light and lightning bolts to escape. I wish the dragon could catch this little imp. He is dangerous and very nasty. Are you prepared just in case?"

"I am taking the week off and will be nearby all the time. We have the mirrors and the flashlights ready and we carry our sunglasses all the time. I also have my big baseball bat ready, so if I can get a shot at him, he'll feel the power of a bat on his head."

Sara smiled. Her brother had always been the family protector with his bat. Once a squirrel had run into the house and Matt had hit him right back outside. The squirrel was stunned and then ran off into the woods. In high school he put the bat to good use on the baseball team and hit a record number of homeruns. He knew how to use a bat.

As they entered they each grabbed some of Katie's cookies. Sara took the twins to the living room while Jim helped Matt with the suitcases. Katie sat on the sofa with Sara and held one of the twins. "We'll take good care of Zoe and George and never let them out of our sight."

"I know you will, Katie. You are the best. Have you seen the dragon yet?"

"I really want to, but nothing yet. I know he is around because Matt talks to him, but I just haven't been able to see him."

"Perhaps this visit will help. You just have to believe and it takes time."

Everyone enjoyed the afternoon watching the eagles from the deck, feeding the squirrels on the railing, and putting together a big puzzle on the kitchen table. Aunt Katie served her delicious lasagna for dinner. Then the children said goodbye to their parents and the twins, and Sara and Jim headed home with the little ones. Zoe and George helped Katie clean up the kitchen and then they climbed into bed.

"Can we go to the chasm tomorrow? We haven't been there since last summer. Remember all those stories you told us about the fairies? I know we are going to see them this time." Zoe had been waiting all year to return to the chasm near the river house. The chasm was a large crack between the rocks that had been formed millions of years ago. It had a beautiful stream flowing down the rocks and ferns and trees everywhere. It seemed the perfect place for fairies to live.

Aunt Katie had grown up on a nearby farm and she said she visited the chasm often as a little girl. She couldn't remember if she had ever seen any fairies, but she was pretty sure they were make-believe. George held her hand and told her, "Aunt Katie, you have to believe. You can't see these things even when they are right in front of you if you don't believe. They are real. Trust me."

Katie said she would really try and they could visit the chasm tomorrow afternoon. She kissed them good night and joined Matt to discuss how they would protect the children. "I talked to the dragon and he will put a protection spell around our house. That will keep everyone safe at night. But he said the flowing water in the river disrupts spells on the land, so he couldn't protect everywhere around the house. We'll need to be vigilant whenever they are outside."

They settled down for a good night's sleep. But a red light hovered above the house and then flew up and down the river. It tried to get to the house, but each time it was repelled. Finally the red light flew off into the forest.

* * * * * * * * * * * *

After a hearty breakfast and a long game of hide and seek all over the big house, Zoe and George settled down to read some of their books. They had agreed to read at least one hour every day, and once they were into their books, the hour easily stretched to two or three. Before they knew it, Aunt Katie was calling them to a yummy lunch of grilled cheese sandwiches with pickles.

"This is my favorite lunch," George told her.

"Mine, too," Zoe chimed in. "Do we get to go to the chasm today?"

Matt replied, "Yes, but there are some rules. Since we are on the lookout for this red guy, you can't wander off. You have to stay near us."

"Agreed. We don't want to have anything to do with that red leprechaun. I remember how mean he was in the temple. George and I stared him down and it was such a relief when the dragons locked him up. I wonder how he got loose."

"According to the dragon, some of the green leprechauns tricked Pedraic into wishing that he did not have to guard the box. They granted the wish and that is how the red guy got loose."

After lunch they put water and some snacks in their backpacks and off they went to the chasm. It was only a ten minute walk through the woods and then the deep canyon opened up. The four hiked up into the ferns and the rocks and the stream. It was beautiful.

George spoke first. "This reminds me of that book that Aunt Katie has been reading to us about fairies. This looks just like the place in the book. I think even some of the rock formations are the same."

Katie explained that the book had been written by a local author long ago. Even as an old man he continued to insist the fairies really lived here. Not many people knew about the chasm, so it was pretty much a secret place.

"Doesn't the book say that fairies are lost children who are turned into fairies to protect them from evil?"

As they climbed the stream trail to the end of the chasm Katie explained that according to the legend, the fairies were lost children who were given magical powers. Once they became fairies they could not change back into children, so they became the protectors of children.

The four decided to sit on one of the big rocks to rest and enjoy their snacks. At first they thought they were under attack by dragonflies. Big bugs were flying in their faces and bumping into their ears. George grabbed one instead of swatting at it. When he opened his hand he couldn't believe his eyes.

"Zoe! Look! It's a fairy!"

Everyone looked at George's hand. There was a small girl sitting in his palm, dressed in a blue outfit. She was pointing her finger at George and making all kinds of squeaking sounds. She appeared to be angry and she was scolding him. Then she stood up on his hand. Instead of squeaking she slowed down and said, "You must leave right now. That red guy is snooping around and he will find the chasm soon. You are in danger."

Then she flew up into the trees and the other "dragonflies" flew with her.

"All right you two. Let's move out now." Matt picked up George and Katie took Zoe's hand. They moved down the trail quickly.

"Did you see them, Aunt Katie? Did you see them?"

Katie was weeping with tears of joy. "I saw them, George. And now I remember that I often visited this chasm as a child and the fairies were my friends that I would play with. They were my dragon."

Everyone was relieved when they reached the house. They ran inside and settled down on the sofas. "Uncle Matt, when is this all going to end? George and I can't be in hiding forever. It just isn't fair."

"Zoe, I am sure the dragon and your parents are trying really hard to catch this leprechaun. You and George can help us best by following the rules we have set up without any arguments. As much as I know you wanted to stay in the chasm and meet those fairies, you were both good to leave immediately without any complaints. I am going to call your folks now and explain what happened." Matt left the room.

"Aunt Katie, you saw them! You see, you can do it. Just believe."

"And I can't believe what I am seeing on my deck right now. A huge green dragon. Matt....Honey.... He's here."

A Day at the Beach

It was a beautiful Saturday morning in late August. George and Zoe jumped out of bed and raced to the window. "What a great day to go see the dragon. We only have a week left before school starts, so now is the time to have some fun." They dressed quickly and scampered down to breakfast.

Sara had prepared their favorite yogurt with blueberries and some warm oatmeal muffins with lots of melted butter. They washed it all down with big glasses of orange juice. "What's on your agenda for today?" she asked.

"We told the dragon we wanted to go to the beach before school starts. He said we should bring our bathing suits and towels, so we are ready to go."

"I hope you have a good time. Be sure to put on sunscreen and be careful in those waves. Follow the dragon's directions exactly."

"Thanks, Mom. We know how to follow his rules and we will be very careful. No need to get hurt right before school starts."

The children hustled out the back door and ran to the tree. They knocked three times and the door opened. They slid down the spiral staircase railing and raced up the yellow path. Zoe arrived first and knocked on the dragon's door.

"Come in, children. How are you today? Are we ready to go to the beach?"

"Oh yes, Mr. Dragon! We are ready."

"Then pack the sandwiches and water and let's get going."

George got the backpacks and the water while Zoe made the PB&J sandwiches. The children changed into their bathing suits so they would be ready to swim. Everything was packed up with the towels and sunscreen and they climbed aboard the dragon's back. "Let's go!"

They flew up into the clouds and within minutes they descended to a beautiful beach on the Florida coast. George exclaimed, "I wish we could get to Florida this quick all the time. The drive is so long."

The dragon drifted down to a quiet part of the beach. First, they set up a big tent for shade and then they put on their sunscreen. "We're ready to hit the ocean," Zoe announced.

"All right, children. Here are the rules. You must stay within fifty feet of the tent unless I am with you. The tent has a protection spell on it. No swimming without me either. The leprechaun probably doesn't know we are here, but we can't take any chances. Agreed?"

They chimed in together, "Agreed."

The three danced down to the water's edge and the big waves came crashing in on their feet. They laughed and splashed about. Zoe and George climbed onto the dragon's back and he swam way out into the water. They surfed on his back several times, floating on top of the waves. Finally, Zoe said she was tired and wanted to rest. George agreed and the dragon was glad to hear it. He was tired, too.

They went back to their tent and spread out their picnic lunch. As always, Zoe had packed a wonderful collection of yummy delights including lots of fruits and her PB&J sandwiches stuffed with jelly. After lunch they settled down for an afternoon nap inside the tent and they heard people screaming and they sat up right away.

Adults were yelling, "There's a bear on the loose! What is he doing at the beach? Everybody run for their cars. Hurry!"

The dragon looked out of the tent at the beach. There was a large bear running down the beach towards them with several large crabs chasing after him. He looked scared. The dragon stepped out of the tent and asked the bear what was so scary about some little crabs. The bear yelled back, "It's not the little ones I am worried about. It's that big one over there."

The dragon looked further down the beach and saw a huge crab over six feet tall scurrying up the beach. The crab was chasing the bear clearly looking for a big lunch. When the small crabs saw the dragon they all ran into the water and swam away. But the big crab did not even pay attention to the dragon and continued to chase after the bear. The dragon stepped between them and told the crab to stop. The crab skidded to a stop on the sand and eyed the dragon.

The dragon pointed his claw at the crab. "You need to go back into the ocean and leave this bear alone. You don't eat bears."

The crab replied, "I'll eat anything I want and this bear looks particularly yummy to me. And you will make a fine dessert." As the crab lunged at the dragon, he stepped to the side, and the crab never touched him.

"I am going to warn you one last time, you need to leave us alone."

The giant crab rose on his hind legs and lunged at the dragon again. The dragon blew a fiery blast at the crab and it was instantly cooked, stuck in the sand. George and Zoe ran out of the tent and were amazed at the huge crab.

"I had no choice, children. The crab would not back off."

"I heard you warn him twice. You gave him the chance to run away. Too bad for him, Mr. Dragon."

The dragon lifted the crab and threw it far out into the ocean. The bear had disappeared and the beachgoers were coming back to their blankets and umbrellas. George asked if they could build a sand castle before they flew home. Zoe and the dragon agreed and the three built a huge castle over ten feet tall. It looked like a real castle. Just as they finished the last tower, a huge wave came onto the beach and washed away the castle. All that was left was a pile of wet sand.

George laughed, "That's what always happens to my sand castles. We'll come back again another day to build another one. Thanks, guys!"

They packed up the tent, the towels and beach toys, and climbed onto the dragon's back. They flew up into the clouds and shortly descended into the cave. Everyone got cleaned up from the sand and salty water and then they enjoyed some of the dragon's chocolate chip cookies and milk.

"This was an incredibly fun day, Mr. Dragon. Thank you so much."

"Yeah, and thanks for helping me with my sand castle."

"And thank you, children, for following the rules and making a delicious lunch. I can't wait to go again."

"I wanted to ask you if that leprechaun has finally given up and will leave us alone?"

"I am sorry to say that he is still around. I had another encounter with him last night at the temple. He wants all the gold. I will figure something out. Just be on your guard. Say hello to your mom and dad and the twins."

The children ran down the yellow pathway, up the spiral staircase, and out of the tree. They dashed across the yard to the kitchen door and burst into the house.

"We had the best time at the beach!" George exclaimed.

Sara was feeding Annie and Nate and turned to greet them. She pulled out her journal and said, "Tell me all about it."

<u>Trouble at the Zoo</u>

It was a beautiful Saturday morning in September and Zoe and George jumped out of bed and ran to the window. They had been in school now for two weeks and it was time to visit the dragon and share all their news. Zoe was starting fourth grade and George had moved to third. They dressed quickly and raced down the stairs to breakfast.

"Good morning, sleepy heads. What are the plans for today?"

"Time to visit the dragon and tell him all about school. How are the twins?"

"They are doing great and it is a relief that they are sleeping more during the night. I think we are all getting more sleep."

The children finished their delicious breakfast, waved goodbye to their mom, and raced out to the tree. They knocked three times, the door opened, they slid down the railing to the yellow path, and ran the whole way to the dragon's doorway. George knocked and yelled, "Good morning, Mr. Dragon!"

"Hello, children, how are you doing? How is school?"

George began telling the dragon all about third grade. He loved his teacher and all his best friends were in his class. He enjoyed the work and especially the history lessons about his home state, Maryland. School was great and he couldn't wait for Monday morning.

"And Ms. Zoe, what about you?"

"It is so much better than last year. My teacher is really smart and he asks us so many challenging questions. I love the really hard math that I am learning and the boys have stopped the teasing. In fact, some of them are asking me to help them with their math homework. That's a switch. And I have two close girlfriends and we are doing a lot together. Life couldn't be better."

"I am so glad to hear that all is going well. And the babies are growing up?"

George replied, "Well, I don't know about growing up, but at least they are sleeping through the night and have stopped crying so much. Annie and Nate are really cute and they are learning how to eat real food. They smush it all over their faces and squeeze it in their fists. It is so funny to watch!"

"And of course, George is encouraging them to do it and even trying it himself. Can you imagine Mr. Dragon, a grown boy smushing his food in his fists?" Zoe smiled and giggled at George. He returned the smile. The dragon chuckled.

"It's fun to have an excuse to play with the food, especially the yucky vegetables."

"So what do you want to do today? The weather looks perfect for a trip to somewhere exciting."

"I have to do a report on animals for my science class. A trip to the zoo would really help me out," Zoe shared.

"All right, the zoo," George said. "We really need to go to the monkey house. They are so funny to watch. And the elephants are so big. Let's go."

"Very good then. Let's prepare and head out."

Zoe and George did the customary preparations with food and water in their backpacks. When all was ready, they climbed aboard the dragon and flew out of the cave and up into the clouds. Soon they descended to the National Zoo and landed near the tiger enclosure. There were six white tigers in the compound. Some were sleeping and some were licking their fur like cats. One was pacing back and forth on a long log, looking right at Zoe and George.

"I don't like the looks of that tiger," George said. "What is he staring at?"

Before the dragon could answer, the tiger rose up on the log and growled at the children. "I wish you were a little closer so I could have you for my lunch. You look so tasty. Wouldn't you like to climb over the fence and join me in here?" The tiger's eyes glowed red.

"Look away!" Zoe yelled. She pulled out her sunglasses and pushed George down on the ground. The dragon turned away.

"Okay, Zoe. I get it. The leprechaun creep is inside the tiger somehow. I've got my sunglasses on."

Then the dragon pointed his claw at the tiger and the tiger fell asleep on the log. A red light sped away from the tiger and rose high up into the clouds. "I'll be back." They could hear the leprechaun's evil laugh as he disappeared into the sky.

"When will we be rid of this creep?"

"That is the first time he has shown himself in many weeks. I am meeting with the Dragon Council tonight to devise a trap to catch him. We'll work on it. I think he is gone for now, so let's enjoy the zoo."

The three wandered through the zoo and enjoyed learning about the animals. Zoe took notes and photos for her report while George made faces and played with the monkeys through the big windows in the monkey house. They saw beavers, prairie dogs, antelope, lions, and even an anteater. Zoe filled her notebook with information.

After a long day at the zoo, they were preparing to fly home when they heard someone yell, "The elephant is loose. Look out, he is really mad and he is running about. Run for your lives!"

While everyone else ran away from the elephant, the dragon told Zoe and George to sit still and he ran towards the elephant. When he reached the elephant house, he found the gate hanging open and saw the big elephant running down the path. He flew over the elephant and landed in front of him. "I think you need to turn around and go back. You don't want these humans to get crazy and hurt you in some way."

The elephant laughed. "Every once in a while, I open the gate and run around for a few minutes to get everyone excited. Then I return to the compound. They always give me extra food, especially those yummy sweet watermelons. Don't worry, I don't hurt anyone. I'm headed back to the house now." The elephant turned and ran back to the gate. As he lumbered into the compound, he pulled the gate closed with his tail. The zoo keepers were greatly relieved and piled several large watermelons into his food basket. The dragon let out a hardy chuckle and returned to the children.

As they flew back to the cave he explained what the elephant had done. Zoe and George laughed at the elephant's trick. "He's a pretty smart elephant. I think I will put that in my report."

"Good idea, Zoe. Then everybody will think you can talk to animals." George fell on the floor of the cave rolling in peals of laughter.

"And I'll tell all your friends that you were right there with me, talking to the monkeys. So there, young man." Zoe turned up her nose and winked at the dragon.

They enjoyed a snack at the dragon's big kitchen table and then headed home. "Thanks, Mr. Dragon. That was a lot of fun. See you in a few days."

"Good luck with the report, Zoe."

The children ran down the yellow path, up the staircase, through the tree door, and across the yard. George won the race this time and burst into the kitchen to tell his mother that Zoe was talking to animals.

Sara looked at them with many questions in her eyes. Nate and Annie laughed at George and Zoe and then they smashed some peas on their trays. The children told their mom all about their adventures at the zoo. She enjoyed the part about the elephant. She was not at all happy to hear about the tiger with the red eyes. She wrote it all down in the journal.

The Wild Hawaiian Dragon

It was the last Saturday in September and the children could tell that fall was coming. They jumped out of bed and looked out the window as the sun rose behind the mountain and they could see the first tinges of color on the leaves. Soon the mountain would be a beautiful golden glow of yellow leaves. They got dressed and ran downstairs for breakfast. It was a good day to visit the dragon.

During the week their mom didn't always have time to make fancy breakfasts, but Saturday mornings were always special with pancakes, gooey syrup, fruits and berries, and big glasses of orange juice. As they gulped down their last bites, Sara asked where they were off to today.

George replied, "I have to do some research on Hawaii, so I thought I would ask the dragon to take us there."

"Hawaii? I've never been there. If you get to go, that will be really special. And you must be very careful. The dragons still have not caught this leprechaun."

"We know, Mom. Everywhere we go we keep a watch out. We have our sunglasses with us all the time. I am going to ask the dragon to let me read through his magic books to see if I can find anything to stop this red elf. I am sick and tired of waiting."

"Zoe, I understand, but you must be careful. Don't become impatient. Just stick with the plan and you will be safe. Have fun in Hawaii." Sara gave her children big hugs and sent them on their way out the back door. They skipped across the lawn to the tree, knocked three times, and she saw them disappear into the little door in the tree. She knew the dragon would protect her children, but she was still worried.

Zoe and George arrived at the dragon's doorway and knocked. "Come on in, children. How are you today?"

"We're doing just great and we want to go to Hawaii so I can get some information for my report."

"Hawaii, George? I haven't been there in some time. Sounds like fun. Is there anything in particular that you need to see?"

"I want to see a volcano and maybe some jungle stuff. That should be enough."

"Well, if we are going all that distance, then I want to see the beaches and the waves. Aren't there great surfers there? And I think the flowers are supposed to be spectacular. And pineapple, too."

"Zoe, we don't have time to see flowers and fruits. I'd like to see the surfing. That sounds like fun."

"Then let's get going to Hawaii. Prepare all the supplies and off we will go."

Within minutes they were flying high in the clouds and then descending towards some green islands in the middle of the ocean. "Whoa! This is beautiful! Look at the blue ocean, the huge waves, and the volcanoes."

"Let's see what we can find." The dragon flew towards one of the islands and spotted a large field of pineapples. They landed in the middle of the farm.

"Look at all these pineapples. There are zillions of them. What funny looking plants."

George took several pictures of the pineapple plantation. As he was clicking away Zoe and the dragon walked through the field. They heard a faint voice screaming far away. "Help! He's going to get me! Help!"

George came running and the children jumped on the dragon's back. "We must find out who is in trouble." They flew up over the fields and Zoe saw a girl running across a grassy meadow. There was a large black dragon chasing after her. The dragon was yelling at the girl. "You stop stealing my flowers. Get off of my property. Get out of here."

At first the children thought the girl needed saving, but after hearing the dragon's complaints, they weren't sure who was in the wrong. Mr. Dragon flew down and landed between them. The black dragon and the girl both stopped and stared at the children on the back of a green dragon.

The black dragon asked them who they were and why they were on his land. He was pretty rude and bossy. Mr. Dragon replied, "We mean no harm. We are visiting from far away and heard the screaming. Is there anything we can do to help?"

The girl and the dragon tried to talk at the same time. The messages were garbled. "You can leave my land." "You can get rid of that mean dragon." "You can take that little brat away, she steals my flowers." "They aren't his flowers. He doesn't own anything around here."

Zoe clapped her hands loudly and shouted, "All right, you two. Enough." The girl and the dragon were silent. "We didn't travel all this way to see you two fighting. Little girl, explain this quietly, and then the black dragon will get his turn."

The girl explained that her grandfather owned the farm and she collected flowers each day to make leis to sell to the tourists. The dragon had no business on her grandfather's farm and he should leave.

The black dragon then explained that he had lived on this farm for a thousand years and nobody had ever bothered him until this little girl came along stealing his flowers. He had worked for a long time collecting and growing the flowers. She was a thief in his gardens.

George asked, "Why can't you two just get along here? There are tons of flowers and if you would just pick the ones that the dragon says you can, you should be able to share. What is the big deal?"

The black dragon glared at George. "This is none of your business, little boy. The little girl is mine to deal with." The dragon grabbed the girl in his claws and flew away towards one of the volcanoes. The children told Mr. Dragon to follow him and they flew after the black dragon.

The Hawaiian dragon was fast and he flew back and forth through the jungle and along cliffs and down into valleys. But Mr. Dragon kept a steady pace and followed him all the way. They arrived at the top of a volcano.

The black dragon yelled, "Time to get rid of you, you little brat!" He held the girl out over the volcano opening and released her. She fell down into the volcano cauldron. Mr. Dragon dove at lightning speed and caught the girl before she reached the molten lava. He flew back out of the cauldron and put the three children on a cliff to one side. "Stay here," he ordered.

Mr. Dragon rose up to face the black dragon. "Dragons do not harm children. You could have just as easily dropped her off at her house as into a volcano. What is wrong with you?"

"There's nothing wrong with me, buddy. You're trespassing and you're interfering where your big nose does not belong."

"Who is the Master Dragon for Hawaii? I know he will not tolerate this behavior."

"I don't answer to any Master Dragon. He told me that the land belonged to the girl's family and I would have to leave. I told him to forget that and I didn't have to listen to him anymore. He banished me from the dragon clan. That's no big deal to me."

"That may well be, but now that you are harming children, you have two choices. You will stop threatening children."

"Or?"

"Or, you will answer to me. I do not permit any dragon to harm children."

The Hawaiian dragon stood in the air to his full height as if he were trying to scare the children's dragon. Even all puffed out he couldn't meet Mr. Dragon's size even half way.

"All right, I'll leave the little brat alone. You can take the child back to her house. Bye, bye."

Mr. Dragon eyed him suspiciously and then turned to get the children. He could see in Zoe's eyes that something was going on behind him. He turned and dodged to the side just as the other dragon shot lightning bolts at him and blew his strongest fire at him. Mr. Dragon rose up and grabbed the dragon around the neck.

"You have attacked your last dragon!" Then Mr. Dragon threw the black dragon down into the red lava of the volcano. The dragon sank quickly into the molten rock and disappeared.

Mr. Dragon flew over to the cliff.

"Children, I'm so sorry that you had to see that. I avoid violence at all costs."

"Mr. Dragon, you didn't have any choice. He attacked you and tried to kill you. Sometimes when all else fails you have to stand up for yourself and others. Thank you for protecting us from that bully."

The dragon apologized again and then flew the children down into the valley. He let the little girl off at her farm and wished her well. She thanked them for saving her from the mean dragon. Then the dragon and the children flew up into the sky and searched for the beaches. They glided down to the warm sand and watched the surfers slide across the tops of huge waves. They even tried surfing on the dragon's back a few times. The water was a beautiful bluish green.

After enjoying the waves, the dragon said it was time to go. The children climbed aboard and they flew up into the clouds and headed home. They floated into the cave and the dragon let out a big sigh. Zoe and George each took one of the dragon's claws. "You had no choice, Mr. Dragon. If you hadn't acted, we would all be dead. You did the right thing." The dragon nodded his head and said again that he was sorry they had seen that.

After some cookies and milk, Zoe and George hugged the dragon and thanked him for a great trip to Hawaii. They raced down the yellow path, up the stairs, out of the tree, and into the kitchen.

"Mom, you won't believe what happened today." Zoe went on to tell her mom all about the trip to Hawaii and how their dragon had to protect them from another bully dragon. Sara was relieved to know that the dragon had been there for her children. She recorded the story in her journal and Zoe and George entertained the twins while everyone got ready for dinner.

<u>New York City</u>

It was mid-October and the days were still warm in the sun but the evenings were turning cooler and there was even one night of frost. Everyone knew winter was coming and they were preparing for cold weather ahead. George and Zoe awoke to a very rainy Saturday morning with thick gray clouds. "Not such a good day to be outside."

"Nope, George, looks like an inside day at the dragon's cave. Let's get going."

The children got dressed and raced down to breakfast. Mom had been busy and she had baked a wonderful coffee cake covered with that white syrupy frosting. They enjoyed scrambled eggs and big pieces of the coffee cake. The twins were trying their first eggs and they were enjoying stuffing the eggs in their mouths. Zoe asked for a second piece of the coffee cake and George was right behind her as their mom cut more pieces.

"That was great, Mom! Thanks. We're off to see the dragon. See you for dinner."

"Zoe, don't forget that you are watching Ellie's little dog this weekend. I think you will need to take the dog with you to the cave. I am sure the dragon won't mind."

"Oh yeah, I almost forgot that little dog. George, grab Ellie Junior and bring her along." George picked up the little dog and carried it towards the back door.

"I would suggest that you take your raincoats and remember your sunglasses, too. Even in the rain you will need them if the leprechaun returns." The children agreed and headed for the tree. Sara sat at the table watching them go. The red leprechaun had not been seen in many weeks and the dragon council thought he had given up. Zoe assured her mom that the red leprechaun would never give up without a fight. Sara knew this too and had talked to Mr. Dragon about it. He said he also knew that this was not over. He was doing a lot of research and he thought he might have found something to solve the problem. Sara was encouraged to hear this, but still on guard every day. She busied herself taking care of the twins while dreaming of the happy times she had spent with the dragon when she was little.

The children reached the dragon's cave. "Good morning, children. There is a lot of rain out there today. What shall we do?"

Zoe stepped forward and said, "I think it is time for us to do some research in your library and find out how we are going to handle this leprechaun. How about we spend the day going through your books?"

The dragon's eyes opened wide and he gave her a big smile. "I have been doing just that, Zoe. And I think I may have found something. One of the books mentioned a pot of special gold coins in a vault in New York City that is supposed to overpower leprechauns and take away their powers when they touch a coin. Are you interested in going to New York today?"

"You bet we are. And we'll take Ellie's little dog along. Maybe she can find the vault for us."

The dragon looked at Ellie Junior. "She's cute, but I don't think she will be much help. Be sure to put a leash on her. New York City is a big place."

They prepared all the supplies for the trip. Zoe and George put on their backpacks and George grabbed Ellie Junior and they climbed aboard the dragon. They flew out of the cave and up into the clouds. Soon they were above the rain and the sky was blue. The clouds looked like big puffs of marshmallow.

"I wish we could walk on clouds. They look so soft," George laughed.

Soon they descended into New York City and landed in Times Square, right in the middle of thousands of people and all the commotion of a big city. They looked up at the tall buildings and then down the long streets. There was so much to see and do. Where would they begin?

"According to the book, there is a secret vault in the Guggenheim Museum of Art gift store. We have to find the museum, get in, and then figure out how to find the vault in the store." The dragon pulled out a map and looked for the museum. George and Zoe were busy watching the crowds. Somehow, Ellie Junior slipped out of George's grasp and ran off down the street.

"Oh no, Ellie Junior has escaped! We've got to find her."

The three raced after the little dog down one of the side streets. Since the dragon was so tall, he could see Ellie Junior and pointed the way for George and Zoe. Ellie Junior was smart enough to stop at the street corner and wait for the light to change and that gave them a chance to catch up. Just as Ellie tried to jump off the curb George grabbed her.

"You need to stay with us. No more running off." George scolded the dog some more and pointed his finger in her face. She licked his finger and smiled. "I don't know that it was such a good idea to bring this dog!" He put the leash on her to be sure she couldn't run away again.

"Ah, but Ellie Junior has brought us to Fifth Avenue and the art museum is on Fifth Avenue at 89th Street. We are headed in the right direction. Climb aboard and we will fly up Fifth Avenue. Look for a big round building. The museum looks like a big cereal bowl."

They flew up Fifth Avenue taking in all the sights. There was the skating rink at Rockefeller Plaza. Zoe reminded George that they had seen that on a Christmas television program where they lit a big tree. They saw the FAO Schwartz toy store and begged the dragon to stop. "Right now we have to find the vault. If there is time we can return to the toy store."

Then a huge park appeared right in the middle of the city. "That's Central Park," George explained. "There is plenty of cool stuff in there like a zoo and lakes to float boats on. We should go there."

"Not now, George. We have to find the vault at the Guggenheim."

Then Zoe saw the cereal bowl building. "There it is! Sure is a funny-looking building. What do they have inside of it?"

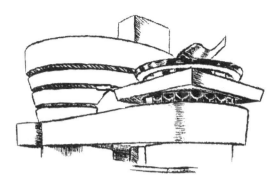

"There is a wonderful collection of modern art, some of the best in the whole world. I think you should tie Ellie Junior to a tree over there and then go up to the window and purchase two tickets. You and George go in the entrance and then I will join you in the lobby. See you there." Zoe and George got their tickets and went through the entrance. They found the dragon looking at a strange sculpture.

"What is that, Mr. Dragon?" George asked.

"It is apparently a mother holding her young child in her lap."

"Uh, I don't see that," Zoe said.

"Well, you have to study it and learn about modern art. It is really fun to try and figure out the art pieces. Look closely. Do you see the mother's head near the top and her arms are these curvy pieces coming around the sides." The dragon was trying to help the children understand the artwork.

George said, "Yeah, I see that. This is really interesting art, the kind of artwork that shows a lot of emotion and creativity. Zoe, you need to read more about it to understand it better."

"George? I didn't know you knew anything about modern art."

"We have been learning about it with the art teacher. She showed us this sculpture a few weeks ago. Didn't you pay attention to the art teacher when you were in third grade?"

Zoe frowned at George. "I guess I didn't listen closely enough."

The dragon remembered why they were at the museum and said, "All right, now we have to find this vault and the pot of gold coins. It is supposed to be located in the Museum Gift Store which is right over there. Hmmmm, the sign says it is closed for renovation. That's not good."

"I think it is great! There won't be anyone to bother you while you search. George and I will walk around for a bit and let you go in the store. You're invisible to most everyone and you can go in and find it."

"You are right, Zoe. I have to hold both my claws out to feel the energy from the vault. As soon as I have the pot of gold coins, I'll find you two."

George took Zoe's hand and led her into one of the galleries. "See this one. The art teacher showed us this last week and explained that the artist wanted the colors to bring out the feelings of a spring afternoon in the forest. Look at all the brilliant green colors. Don't you feel like we are on the mountain climbing to the top?"

Zoe looked at the painting. She squinted and tried to picture the woods. She turned her head side to side and even looked at it upside-down. "George, I just can't see it."

"Zoe, you feel it, you don't see it. It's like believing in dragons. Close your eyes and listen to me." Zoe closed her eyes and concentrated on George's voice. "Pretend you are on the mountain. Listen for the birds, feel the breeze in your hair. Hear our feet rustling in the leaves. Feel the warmth of the sun on your face. See the beautiful green leaves glowing in the sunlight. Now open your eyes."

Zoe looked at the painting again. "Oh, George! I really see what you mean. If you don't look for everything in normal ways, you can imagine them. See, there is a stream and a big rock to sit on to look at the fish in the water. How cool is that?" George stared at the picture and began to see what she was talking about.

The children wandered through the galleries playing with the artwork in their minds, imagining they were in the paintings or talking to the sculptures. Meanwhile, the dragon had slipped into the construction area. He held out his claws and walked through the store. It was just a big open space now since all the cabinets and furniture and items for sale were removed. As he crossed the room, he sensed some energy coming from the right. He followed the energy to the wall and found a small door.

With a flick of his magic claw the door opened and he found a small pot of gold coins. "Ah, just what we need." He picked up the pot and slid it into one of the children's backpacks and carefully closed the door. He left the store and found the children on the third floor, looking at a group of black boxes that were stacked in odd ways. George was explaining to Zoe how they were perfectly balanced. They turned around when the dragon arrived.

"Do you have it?"

"Yes, and it is time for us to go. Let's get the dog outside and head home."

The trio left the museum, picked up Ellie Junior, and flew off to the dragon's cave. When they arrived, they gave Ellie Junior a bowl of water and some crackers. George, Zoe, and the dragon enjoyed their chocolate chip cookies and milk.

"So what do we do with the coins?"

"I will finish reading about them, but I am pretty sure that everyone will need to carry one in case the leprechaun appears. I'll let you know next time we meet. Say hi to your mother."

Zoe and George raced down the yellow path, up the stairway, and out into the backyard. They ran to the kitchen and told Sara what they had found in New York City. She was encouraged to see that the dragon was finally finding a solution to this leprechaun problem. She wondered what these magic coins would do. She would tell Jim about the coins when he got home from work. Sara wrote down the day's adventure in her journal.

Zoe talked with the twins about the dragon and George helped his mother set the table for dinner. When Dad got home they settled down to a yummy spaghetti dinner. Annie and Nate had fun pulling on the strings of spaghetti while getting tomato sauce all over their faces. Everyone laughed.

A Dinosaur in Africa

It was the Saturday before Halloween and the children wanted to show the dragon their costumes. They had decided to dress up like two of the sculptures they had seen in the Guggenheim Art Museum and the costumes really turned out quite good. They jumped out of bed and got dressed and took the bags with the costumes down to breakfast.

Sara had made her special pumpkin pancakes that tasted like pumpkin pie and were shaped like jack-o-lanterns. She even used whipped cream to put the eyes, nose, and mouth on each one. The twins were getting old enough now to begin exploring foods. They enjoyed smooshing blueberries into some whipped cream while Zoe and George ate a scrumptious breakfast. Dad joined the festive meal.

"That was GREAT, Mom. Thanks!" George and Zoe waved goodbye to their mom and headed for the tree with their bags of costumes. Into the tree, down the stairs, up the yellow pathway, and into the cave, they announced that they were here to share their Halloween costumes.

The dragon laughed and asked, "What will you be this year? I don't know how you will top the Super Zoe outfit and the magician from last year."

The children put on their costumes. "Ta-da. Don't I look like that sculpture of a dog chewing on a bone you were talking to in the Guggenheim? And doesn't Zoe look like that mother with her baby?"

The dragon clapped his claws together. "Why yes, I see both of the sculptures. What a great idea." He admired all their handiwork and then helped them get out of the complicated outfits. "What shall we do today?"

"I think it is your turn to choose, Mr. Dragon. Where would you like to go?"

"I haven't been to Africa in a long time and I hear that they may have found a dinosaur in the jungles."

"You mean dinosaur bones, right?"

"No, George, they claim they have seen a real Tyrannosaurus roaming through the jungles. The natives are really scared."

"But all the dinosaurs are extinct. They couldn't possibly have found one. What do you think it really is?"

"Perhaps someone's Halloween costume," the dragon chuckled. "I think we should go and investigate."

"Sounds good to me," Zoe said. "Let's get all the supplies and our jungle hats."

When all was ready, the children climbed aboard the dragon and flew out of the cave. They could see their house down in the valley and the sun was shining on their tree fort in the big tree. The view was breathtaking.

In just a few minutes they were flying over Africa and searching for the jungle where the dinosaur had been seen. The dragon spread out his claws searching for dinosaur energy and after a while he pointed to a clearing near the top of a big mountain. They glided down to the grassy area and landed on a big rock.

"How do you know this is the right place?"

"I used my magic to feel the energy of a very large animal. If the dinosaur is not here, something else is that is very big. Keep a close watch because I am not sure how to handle a dinosaur."

They sat on the rock for about a half an hour and the dragon kept putting his claws out to feel energy. "It is very strong in that direction." He pointed to a clump of trees below them.

Then they heard loud thumps on the ground as if a giant were walking through the jungle and everything was shaking. Trees were falling down and some were flying up into the air. Birds were flying about wildly and several monkeys, an elephant, and two tigers came running out of the jungle. Something was tearing up the jungle and the animals were frantic to escape. The tigers ran by their rock without even noticing them.

The pounding thumps came closer and the trees at the edge of the clearing were shaking. Then some of the trees fell and others flew to the side. A massive lizard that looked like a Tyrannosaurus was standing in the trees. His big yellow eyes were focused on the children. They sat with their mouths open. The dragon grabbed them both and put them on his back.

"Time to go." He shot straight up into the clouds just as the lizard ran at the rock. They were well above him when he crashed head first into the boulder. The lizard shook his mighty head back and forth and then fell down. He had knocked himself out.

The dragon carefully flew down to get a closer look at the unconscious lizard. It certainly looked like a Tyrannosaurus, but something was not quite right. Why would an animal have a door on its back? Why would smoke be coming out of a lizard's feet? The dragon approached from behind and tapped the lizard with his claw. It rang out like metal. Dinosaurs did not have metal skin. The dragon landed and the three cautiously walked up to the lizard.

"It's a machine, Mr. Dragon. It's not really a dinosaur. Why would anybody make a robot like this?"

The door on the back of the lizard opened and a bald man stuck his head out. He was straightening his thick black-rimmed glasses and saying in a whiny voice, "Oh dear....Oh Dear." Then he crawled out of the doorway and sat on the lizard. "How am I going to get this fixed? The boss is going to be so mad at me. Why didn't I see that rock?"

Zoe called out, "Hey, what are you doing with that thing?"

The man could only see the children and he was very surprised that anyone was around. "Where did you come from?"

"We just fell out of the sky and wanted to see this dinosaur," said George. "But it doesn't appear to be real."

The little man in his white coat said, "We mustn't tell anyone about this. This is going to be our little secret, children. Why don't you come over here and tell me more about how you got here?" He began to climb down the lizard towards them. "This is a science experiment. You know about science experiments from school, don't you? Now come over here."

Zoe looked at George and then turned to the dragon. "It's time to get out of here. This guy is weird and I don't trust him."

"I agree." The dragon scooped the children up with his claws and placed them on his back. He took them up into the clouds and headed home. The little man in his white coat and black glasses stared at the two children flying through the sky. The natives believed in his Tyrannosaurus, but he was sure nobody would ever believe him if he said he saw two children flying. He sat down on the rock with his head in his hands as the children disappeared.

The trio flew home and settled into the cave. "That was really weird. What was that man trying to do?"

"I'm not sure, but I'll do some research and check him out," said the dragon. "Even if the dinosaur is a robot, I don't think it would be good for that thing to be on the loose. Look what it did to the jungle."

They talked more as they enjoyed their cookies and milk. Then the dragon handed each of them a gold coin. "Carry this with you always. If you are cornered by the leprechaun, offer it to him as payment. As soon as he touches it he will lose his powers and then you can run away. I will be giving coins to your parents and uncles and aunts as well. They should protect everyone.

"I will also be following you two tonight on your Halloween adventures. I don't think the leprechaun will come out since he won't be able to figure out who you are in all the costumes. But we will be prepared just in case."

The children thanked the dragon for the protection coins and for the fun trip to Africa. They ran down the yellow path, up the spiral staircase, out of the tree, and across the yard. When they reached the kitchen, they told Sara all about the magic coins. She was relieved to see those coins and called Jim into the kitchen to see them. Then George and Zoe described the crazy trip to Africa, and Sara wrote it all down in the journal.

The Dairy Farmer

It was the weekend after Halloween. George and Zoe had collected so much candy that they could eat it for weeks. They shared it with their parents, too. But the twins were too young to eat sweets, so the children were perfectly happy not sharing with them. George packed a bag of chocolates for the dragon and they raced down to breakfast.

"It was kind of a long night with the babies, so do you mind cereal this morning?" Sara looked pretty tired and Jim was still in bed.

"Cereal is fine. We can get it. Why don't you go back to bed and get some sleep while you can. We'll be with the dragon."

"Have fun. I am definitely going back to bed." Sara left the kitchen and Zoe and George made their breakfast. When they finished they put the dishes in the sink and dashed out the door to the tree. Three knocks and they were on their way to the cave. As they entered the cave, they found the dragon sitting in his chair reading a big book.

"Good morning, children. I am finishing my research on the leprechaun. I found out that the robot dinosaur was a big hoax that a crazy scientist put together. He wanted to scare away everyone in the area so he could mine some rare mineral. He built the dinosaur robot, but it never occurred to him that people from all over the world would come looking for a dinosaur. Anyways, the police in Africa locked him up and took the dinosaur robot to a local museum."

George handed the dragon the chocolates as he said, "Yeah, I read about him on the Internet. He sounds really nuts. Glad we got away from him. What about the leprechaun?"

"The coins will work. They probably won't take away his powers forever, but they will temporarily stun him so a person can escape or capture him. If he shows up again, we will get him."

George said, "That's good. I'm glad we have these coins. I hope we can catch this leprechaun and get rid of him.

"I met a new boy at school who lives on a nearby farm. Can we go visit him today? He raises dairy cows and they make real ice cream at his farm."

"Ice cream? Let's go!" Zoe and the dragon were grinning from ear to ear.

The trio flew out of the cave and glided down the valley looking for Jack's dairy farm. When they saw it they landed in the driveway and George went up to the front door and rang the bell. Jack answered and said he would be right out. A few minutes later, Jack came out of the door with his BB gun.

"I'm going to hunt some squirrels for dinner."

"You are going to shoot squirrels?! And then eat them?!" Zoe asked with big eyes.

"Naw, I was just kidding. I shoot tin cans off of the fence posts. Come on and I'll let you try." Jack began to lead the way when he saw the dragon. "What....Who... What is that?"

George told Jack, "That is our friend, Mr. Dragon. He lives on the mountain and we do all kinds of fun things with him."

Jack raised his BB gun and aimed it at the dragon. "I don't like any big lizard coming on to my father's dairy farm. They like to eat cows you know."

Zoe jumped in front of the gun. "Put that down, NOW! This dragon isn't going to hurt you or any of your silly old cows."

"Get out of the way, Zoe. I don't want to hurt you but I can't have lizards around here," Jack said.

George put his hand on his friend's shoulder. "It's all right, Jack. He is friendly and he isn't going to hurt any of your cows." The dragon smiled at Jack. Jack lowered his BB gun.

"Well, okay, but he better not get out of line or I'll kapow him."

Zoe stood her ground between Jack and the dragon. "If you are going to continue to threaten him, we're leaving. I don't like people who are mean to our dragon."

Jack lowered his head. "I'm sorry. I didn't mean to hurt any feelings. I've never seen anything like this before. What do you mean you go on adventures?"

Zoe and George climbed up on the dragon's back and then invited Jack to join them. He put his BB gun back on the porch and then he cautiously approached the dragon and climbed up next to them.

"Welcome aboard, Jack," the dragon said. "You can join us on some of our trips if you like. Would you like to fly above your farm?"

"You can fly? All right!"

"I take it that is a yes. Off we go." The dragon flew above the farm and swooped down over the ponds and glided along the fields near the cows. The cows would moo at them as they flew by. It was an exhilarating flight over the dairy farm.

When they landed, Jack let out a loud whoop. "That was unbelievable! Come on, you deserve some ice cream. Just don't scare my mom and dad."

"You need to know that grown-ups can't see the dragon. They don't believe, so they can't see him. The less you talk about him with your parents, the better for you.

Adults want to constantly tell you that you are imagining things."

"I get it. This is our secret. It is so cool to know a dragon. Thanks!"

They all enjoyed big ice cream cones full of freshly made ice cream. Then it was time to head back to the cave. "Some day we'll take you to the cave," George told Jack. "Thanks for the ice cream."

Zoe and George climbed aboard the dragon and waved goodbye to Jack and off they flew towards the mountain and the cave. "He is a nice chap, George. Glad you introduced us to him."

"Thanks, Mr. Dragon. I'm sorry about the BB gun."

"No big deal. He was afraid. I am glad that you and Zoe could explain things to him. I am sure he will add much to our adventures in the future."

The children waved goodbye to the dragon and raced down the yellow path, up the stairs, out of the tree, and across the yard to the kitchen door. Sara was up and looked much better after a few hours of sleep. She wrote down the trip to the dairy farm and told the children she would like to visit the farm for some ice cream, too. "Your father loves homemade ice cream. The twins might even try a little taste. We'll visit soon."

The Dragon's Birthday

It was November eleventh and it was the dragon's birthday. The children had no idea how old the dragon was, but they prepared cards, some presents, and a cake with some candles on it. Sara had helped with the baking. As they jumped out of bed they could feel the chill of winter in the air. Overnight there had been a small snow shower and everything outside was covered in a dusting of snow.

"Brrrr. We better dress warmly today." They got dressed and raced to breakfast. Sara had everything ready for the dragon's party. The children dug into their yummy breakfast of eggs and muffins and then prepared to carry everything to the cave. Sara carried the cake to the tree and handed it into Zoe once she was inside the tree.

"Be sure to take the cake first. There are little varmints living in the tree and the tunnel that will enjoy it for breakfast, so get it to the dragon before you bring the presents. See you all later. Have fun and wish him a Happy Birthday from me." The little door closed and Sara returned to the kitchen.

Zoe carried the cake and George managed the presents. He had to make a second trip to get the big card and the balloons. The dragon was surprised and so pleased that they had remembered his birthday. He sat on his sofa admiring the presents and the cake and the card.

"So, we know that your real name is Edward, but we prefer to call you Mr. Dragon. How old are you, Mr. Dragon?" George asked.

"To tell the truth George, I am not sure. I have lived here on this mountain since your great grandparents built the white house in 1873. Before that I lived in France with your ancestors. That goes back centuries. I guess you could say I am at least a thousand years old."

"That's a lot of candles! We could burn down your cave with that much fire."

"The candles on the cake are just fine. I appreciate that you remembered it was my birthday. That was so kind."

Zoe and George sang Happy Birthday to the dragon and then they enjoyed the cake as the dragon opened his presents. It was so much fun and he talked about each present as if it was the best thing he had ever gotten. When the party was over, they asked if there was some place special the dragon would like to visit.

"Why, yes. I have never been to Hollywood in California. I think it would be fun to see the sights and visit Grauman's Chinese Theater to see all the handprints of the famous movie stars in the sidewalk."

"Then let's get going. I saw that theater on TV and I think that would be fun to see it in person, too."

Everyone prepared for the trip and the children put on their backpacks and climbed onto the dragon. He flapped his wings and off they went way up into the clouds. In no time at all, they flew down into Hollywood. The big sign on the hillside showed them the way.

They landed at the theater and spent over an hour looking at all the handprints and footprints in the cement. George and Zoe did not know all the older movie stars, but they recognized some of the more recent ones. Zoe thought it was a bit funny to stick your hands and feet in wet cement, but it was cool to see handprints from people long ago. Some of the movie stars had big hands. The dragon really enjoyed the visit.

Then they flew over to Universal Studios and saw the movie sets where some of their favorite TV shows were filmed. Zoe located the building where the cartoons were created and they enjoyed seeing how artists created cartoons on computers for their Saturday morning shows. They learned a lot about how to make movies. After several hours of touring around Hollywood, they agreed it was time to head home. The children climbed onto the dragon and off they went.

As they came out of the clouds near the dragon's cave, they saw the red light in the distance. Zoe and George put on their sunglasses immediately and then they told the dragon where the light was going so he wouldn't have to look at it. The red light suddenly disappeared into the Enchanted Forest. Before George could tell the dragon to slow down and turn left, they crashed into a tree. The dragon hit his head on the trunk and was knocked out. The children fell into some bushes and they were okay. They rushed to the dragon's side.

"Mr. Dragon? Are you okay? Mr. Dragon, are you there?"

Slowly the dragon opened his eyes and stared at the children. "Who are you?" he asked.

"I'm Zoe and this is George. What do you mean, who are we?"

"I don't believe we have met. Thank you for waking me up. I think I am supposed to go home? Or maybe stay here in the forest?"

George looked at Zoe and shook his head. "He hit that tree really hard. I think he has amnesia. What are we going to do?"

Zoe stood in front of the dragon's face and looked into his eyes. "Mr. Dragon, you bumped your head and you have temporarily forgotten. I am Zoe and this is George, two of your close friends. We do a lot of things together. Tell me what you remember."

The dragon sat up and began to talk to the children. "I remember that I live in a cave on a mountain. I remember this forest is enchanted. There are magical plants in this forest." The dragon continued for several minutes listing things he could remember. None of them included the children or their families. He could remember some of his magic spells.

George asked, "Do you know anything about amnesia when people bump their heads and forget things?"

The dragon thought for a moment. "It does happen sometimes. I remember that my friend Joe the Dragon lost his memory for a time. I think we gave him some medicinal tea to help his memory come back. Hmmm...yes, I remember it was made from the flowers of the Looper tree, that tree over there with the orange flowers. We put a bunch of those flowers in boiling water and he drank it down. Then he remembered everything."

"George, can you climb up there and collect the flowers? I'll find some water and something to put it in." Zoe started searching in the leaves around the tree.

George climbed the tree and collected a dozen of the large orange flowers. He brought them to Zoe. She had found an old rusty pot and had filled it with water from the blue stream. The dragon looked at the glowing blue water and the bright orange flowers. He had a silly grin on his face and his eyes were really big. "They look so pretty. How nice. Now what should we do?"

"He sure is acting weird. I hope this tea will work."

"Me, too. Crush your flowers into the blue water and then set the pot on this flat rock." George crumpled each flower in his hand and the petals fell into the glowing blue water. As the petals landed on the water they fizzed and disappeared into the liquid. George carried the pot to the flat rock.

"Mr. Dragon, you must warm the pot with your fiery breath. Blow on the pot gently and make the water boil. Practice over there first." Zoe pointed to the stream of glowing blue water.

The dragon took a deep breath and blew out a huge flame of fire. He put his claw over his mouth. "I think that was a little too strong." He tried again to make the flame small by squeezing his lips shut. A few sparks and a lot of smoke came out of his mouth. After several more attempts, he finally could control the flame so that he could warm the pot without melting it. He carefully brought the pot to boil and the petals danced in the blue water.

Zoe counted to one hundred. "That should be long enough. You said that Joe drank the tea. Did you have to say any magic words or do anything else?"

The dragon put his claw to his head. "Hmmm…yes, he had to drink some tea and then say 'remember', then drink some more tea and repeat 'remember' and so on until all the tea was gone. Then his memory came back."

"Then it is time to get started, Mr. Dragon," George said. "Drink slowly and do it right so that you get every memory back."

The dragon drank the tea and repeated the 'remember' chant over and over. When all the tea was gone, he sat back on the flat rock. Zoe and George stared at him.

"Well?"

The dragon shook his head two or three times, back and forth. He closed his eyes and took a deep breath and chanted 'remember' over and over. When he finally opened his eyes, he looked a lot better. "George…Zoe….is everything all right? Did we find that red leprechaun? Where are we?"

Zoe and George hugged the dragon. "Thank goodness you are back. You hit your head on that big tree and you forgot everything. We had to make this special tea and you drank it and got your memory back."

The dragon rubbed his head. "Yes, it does hurt. What happened?"

The children explained the whole story to the dragon and he finally remembered it all. He asked them what had happened to the red light. They explained that it had disappeared right before he hit his head. "We should leave the forest soon. Who knows what he is up to in the dark and deeper parts of the woods."

They waited a few more minutes and then the dragon said he was ready to go back to the cave. The children climbed aboard and off they flew to the cave. Zoe made sure the dragon was okay while George got him an ice pack for his head. Then they waved goodbye and rushed home.

George and Zoe told their mom all about the latest adventure including the part about the dragon's memory and the red light going into the Enchanted Forest.

"I am so glad that you asked the right questions and helped the dragon. You two are really independent adventurers. I wonder if that tea would help humans remember things? Some days I could use some help finding my car keys."

The children chuckled at their mom's question. The twins just cooed and babbled back and forth. Sara shook her head and wrote everything down in the journal.

The Showdown at the Chasm

It was the Wednesday before Thanksgiving and school was closed. This was the day that George and Zoe always helped Aunt Katie make the pies for the big feast. They jumped out of bed, got dressed, and raced down to breakfast. The twins were already in their high chairs playing with their blueberries and oatmeal.

"Man, you guys can sure make a big mess," George said. "Do you actually eat any of the food?" Annie and Nate both laughed and squished some more of their blueberries.

Sara had scrambled up some eggs and prepared some fresh pumpkin muffins. They smelled so good. After devouring a huge breakfast, Zoe and George were ready to go to Katie's. Their dad took them over to Matt and Katie's house. Uncle Matt was out on the river kayaking with some of his friends. Aunt Katie was waiting for her helpers to arrive so they could make the pies.

The children waved goodbye to their dad and ran into the house. They put on their aprons and climbed up on their stools and began mixing all the ingredients. George loved to make the pie dough and then push it into the pie pans to make the crusts. While the pie crust baked, Zoe worked to make the fillings. Aunt Katie supervised the pie makers and within two hours there were three beautiful pies ready for Thanksgiving dinner---pumpkin pie, apple pie, and the family favorite, peanut butter chocolate pie. That was the hardest pie to make and all three of them had worked together to make it just right.

They cleaned up the kitchen, had a quick bite of lunch, and collapsed on the sofas to take naps. It had been a busy morning and they were exhausted. Soon they were all asleep.

* * * * * * * *

Zoe woke up first and stretched. She got up and walked over to the big windows that looked out over the river. She could see the group of kayakers paddling up the river for one more run before they would return home. What a beautiful sight with fall leaves and the flowing river, so peaceful and inviting, so calm. And then she saw it. The red bubble was hovering over the house and the leprechaun was staring right at her. She put on her sunglasses and stared right back at him. He grimaced at her and she frowned at him. It was time to end this.

Zoe quietly woke up George. She whispered that the leprechaun was outside and it was time to use the coins and get rid of him. As George woke up, Zoe wrote a note to Aunt Katie who was sound asleep on the sofa. "Gone to the chasm to catch the leprechaun. We'll be back soon. Love, George and Zoe"

She placed the note on the coffee table and the children quietly left the house. They ran along the path to the chasm as fast as they could. They made sure the leprechaun was following them. He was right behind them in his red bubble as they dashed into the chasm. About twenty feet into the chasm the children turned to face the leprechaun. His bubble came to a stop and hovered in front of them.

Zoe wanted to yell at the leprechaun and tell him to be gone, but she remembered that they had to get him to take the gold coins. She looked at George and said, "Oh no, he followed us, George. I think we are in big trouble." Then she turned to the leprechaun and asked, "What do you want with us? We don't have any gold or anything else of value."

"I plan to use you two as hostages. I will offer to free you if the dragons give me all the gold that is under that temple. I saw it there and I want it all. You will be the bait." Then he sniffed the air and growled. "I smell some gold now. You two have some gold somewhere on you. Show it to me!"

The leprechaun was shouting in a very angry voice. The children could see that he was getting more and more upset. His face was growing redder and his eyes were terrifying. He thrust his hand through the bubble and pointed at them. "Give it up now or things will be really bad for you."

"But my grandmother gave me this gold coin," George whined and held up his coin. "It is so special to me. I don't want to give it up." Zoe pretended to cry and George looked so forlorn.

"Please Mr. Leprechaun, can't we keep these coins from our grandmother?" Zoe begged as she held the coin in the palm of her hand. George did the same.

"You silly little children. You have no need for those gold coins. Your grandmother won't even know that you lost them. Give them to me!" And the leprechaun leaned out of the bubble and snatched the coins from the children's palms.

For a moment nothing happened as the leprechaun pulled his hand back into the bubble. He stared at the coins with his evil eyes and laughed. Then the red bubble began to rise and the leprechaun became very agitated. "Wait! This cannot be happening! I am losing my powers. The bubble has gone crazy and is out of control." The bubble rose quickly up into the sky, higher and higher it flew. Then it burst with a bright red explosion and a loud boom. There was nothing left after the bright flash. The leprechaun was gone.

Zoe and George let out a yelp of joy. They were free at last. The gold coins had worked and everyone would be so proud of them. They couldn't wait to tell Aunt Katie. Thanksgiving would be a huge celebration.

George turned to Zoe. "We did it! We did it!" He paused and stared at Zoe. "Zoe, why are you wearing that funny blue dress and why are your ears pointy and how did you get wings?"

Zoe looked at George. "Oh my goodness, George! You have pointy ears and wings and a funny looking green suit. What has happened?" George grabbed his ears and realized that he was flying in the air. The children were floating in midair when three fairies came flying over to them.

"We saved you," they cheered. "That mean red man was going to hurt you so we turned you into fairies to protect you. You are safe now! We saved you!"

Zoe and George stared at each other. "That was very nice of you to protect us, but we need to get back to being children now. Please change us back."

One of the fairies replied in her sweet high-pitched voice, "Sorry, once a fairy, always a fairy. You can't go back. But you have a beautiful blue dress and you can fly and we will get you some fairy dust so you can do magic tricks. You'll forget about being a child and have so much fun here in the chasm. It's fun to be a fairy."

George said, "You don't understand. We destroyed that red man with our magic coins. We didn't need any help or protection. So it was nice of you to try and help but we didn't need it. You need to change us back right away so we

can go home."

Another sweet fairy voice replied, "Why, you silly fairy. You aren't going home. Don't you see how much fun you are going to have flying around here? This is your new home. Even if we wanted to change you back into children, we can't. Once a fairy, always a fairy." She smiled as she flitted about.

"Yes, you already said that. George, I think we need to fly to Aunt Katie to get some help. Let's go."

"Oh, you can't do that. You have to stay in the chasm. Only your Aunt Katie can leave. Fairies stay here."

Zoe nodded and then took George's hand and started to fly out of the chasm. The fairies all shouted to stop just as Zoe and George hit an invisible wall and then fell to the ground. "What was that?" George shouted as he rubbed the bruise on his forehead.

"I told you that fairies cannot leave the chasm. If you try to go, you will bump into these invisible walls. Just be happy and enjoy flying about and being good little fairies. We were children once, but we have forgotten all about that and love our fairy lives. Come along and have some fun."

The three fairies giggled and smiled and then flew back into the chasm. George and Zoe sat on a rock and tried to figure out what to do.

<u>Once a Fairy, Always a Fairy</u>

Aunt Katie woke with a start. She had been sleeping so soundly. She looked about the room. "George? Zoe? Where are you two?" Then she saw the note on the table. "Oh no! This can't be. They're only children." Katie called Matt immediately and then Sara and Jim. She told them what the note said. "You all need to get here fast and tell Tom and Emily, too. I'm headed to the chasm. I hope I will get there in time."

Katie ran out the door and across the yard to the trail that led to the chasm. When she reached the entrance, she shouted for Zoe and George. There was no answer. She decided to enter the chasm. To protect herself, she put on her sunglasses and held her gold coin in her hand. If that leprechaun was around she was going to show him a thing or two.

As she walked into the chasm, two dragonflies started flying in her face. She shooed them away, but they kept at her. Then one of the dragonflies went into her ear. Katie screamed, but she could hear the tiny voice. "Aunt Katie, it's me, George." Katie stopped swatting the flies and put her hand out. The two dragonflies landed on her hand and she could clearly see that they were two fairies.

"Oh my, I wasn't sure that you fairies really existed. What have you done with Zoe and George?" She listened carefully to the tiny voices.

"We are Zoe and George. We destroyed the leprechaun with the gold coins. They worked and he blew up. But the fairies in this chasm thought we were in trouble so they changed us into fairies to protect us. We told them that we didn't need their help and we wanted to change back, but..."

Katie finished the sentence, "...once a fairy, always a fairy."

"Yeah, that's what they kept saying. We don't want to be fairies and we want to be changed back. What are we going to do?"

"I'm sure I don't have an answer to that. Let me call everyone." Katie stepped out of the chasm but of course George and Zoe could not follow. She decided to do a conference call with Matt, Sara, and Tom. Someone had to know something to do. She placed the call.

"Okay everybody, you are on a conference call. I ran to the chasm and found Zoe and George. They destroyed the leprechaun with the coins."

"Well, that is great! I'm glad the coins worked."

"But we have a huge problem. The fairies thought that George and Zoe were in trouble so they changed them into fairies to protect them from the leprechaun. And the rule about fairies is that once you are changed into one, you can't change back to a child. We need to ask the dragon how to change them back."

Matt said that he had just reached the house and was headed for the chasm. Sara and Jim were entering the driveway and would be right behind Matt. Tom and Emily were driving near the mountain.

Tom said, "We're near Sara's house. We'll try to find the dragon. Sara, what should we do?"

Sara explained that the knothole in the tree fort was a portal to the dragon's cave. They would have to put their hands on the knothole and repeat three times, 'I believe in dragons' and then they would end up at the dragon's cave doorway. "It's a wild ride so be careful."

Katie ended the conference call as Matt came into view. Sara and Jim honked their horn as they parked their car and headed down the trail to the chasm with the twins in their baby carriers. Soon they were all together, staring at two little fairies who looked a lot like Zoe and George.

Sara told her children, "Emily and Tom are trying to reach the dragon for help. I know it will be all right. Just sit tight."

Zoe said that being a fairy wasn't all that bad for a while. She could fly and her blue dress was really pretty. She flew over to Nate and began to sing. Nate laughed and laughed.

"I don't like my green suit. It is too tight and I look silly. And this squeaky little voice isn't much fun either." George was complaining and wanted to end this sooner than later. But he flew over to Annie and she giggled as she watched him fly around her head.

Tom and Emily stopped at the farmhouse. They walked through the yard and climbed up into the tree fort with some effort. The wooden ladder was not built for adults and they had to help each other to keep from falling. They finally reached the floor and climbed into the fort.

"This was a great treehouse. We had tons of fun here. The dragon helped us build it."

Emily and Tom crawled to the knothole. "I think we need to hurry up, Tom. I sure hope this knothole works."

"Hold my hand," Tom said as he reached out to the knothole. Emily held Tom's right hand and he placed his left on the knothole and they said together, "I believe in

dragons…I believe in dragons….I believe in dragons." There was a sudden whoosh of wind and the next thing they could remember was bouncing onto the hard ground outside of the dragon's cave. They stood up and dusted themselves off and knocked on the dragon's door.

"Come on in, children. Are you ready for Thanksgiving?"

Tom and Emily entered the cave. The dragon looked up and was astonished. "You can only be here if there is something very wrong. What has happened?"

Emily quickly explained about the leprechaun and then the fairy spell. At first the dragon was very pleased that the gold coins had taken care of the leprechaun, but when they told him about the fairy spell he looked very grave. "I have never known of anyone who changed back from a fairy into a child. That has always been a one way spell. Once a fairy, always a fairy. We will have to dig deep into the library to see if there is anything we can do." The dragon led the way to the library.

Tom called Sara. "We are in the dragon's cave. He says that no one has ever reversed the fairy spell. We are going to search the library to see if there is any hope."

Sara thought for a minute. "Tell him to get the bright green book on the top right shelf. The title is Fairyland. I read it once when we were visiting him. I remember something in the back about the spell, but I can't remember the details. Find that book. It is our only hope."

Tom ran into the library and found the dragon and Emily already reading through the Fairyland book, page by page, looking for any clues. "Sara said to go to the back. There is something about the fairy spell there."

They flipped the pages to the back of the book and found the spell. The dragon read it carefully, step by step. "Hmmm… it says here that there is only one way to reverse the spell. It takes a special potion of baby's tears mixed with father's curls in honey to change fairies back into children. But it doesn't say what will happen to the children when they change back. Let's take this book to the chasm and meet together to decide our next steps. "

The dragon stepped into the living room. He pointed to his back and said, "Time to get aboard."

Emily looked at Tom. "Does he mean that we are going to fly there on his back?"

"That's exactly what I mean. We don't have time to waste. We must reverse the spell before the sun sets or they may never be able to return. Climb aboard."

Without any more discussion, Emily and Tom climbed onto the dragon's back. They held on tightly as the dragon flew out of the cave and up into the sky. In no time, they glided down to Matt and Katie's house on the river. The dragon flew through the trees to the chasm entrance.

"That was a wild ride!" Tom exclaimed. Emily couldn't decide if she was excited or frightened. They both took a deep breath as they joined the rest of the family.

The dragon took charge. "We are here and we need to decide what to do right away. The sun will set in less than an hour and then they will be fairies forever. We must act now."

"Tell us what to do."

"The potion is a mixture of honey, the father's curls, and babies' tears. Matt, go get the honey and a large pot. And the scissors, too. I'm sorry Sara, but you must get the babies to cry and collect their tears in a cup or something."

"What happens with the potion, Mr. Dragon? You said you didn't know what the consequences might be."

"We have never brought a child back from the fairy spell. It may work perfectly, or it may affect George and Zoe in some way. I don't know."

"If we don't do the spell, we know they will be fairies forever." The dragon nodded his agreement. "If we do the spell, the children should return, but they may be altered in some way."

Jim said, "I think that is a chance we have to take. Better altered than not at all."

Sara agreed, "I want my children back and we will handle anything that comes of it. Emily, come help me with the babies." Sara and Emily took the babies back to the house. Matt went with them to get the honey and the pot.

A few minutes later he came running with the supplies for the spell.

"Let's get started. Jim, we will need some of your hair."

Jim leaned over and Matt clipped off three locks of his hair and dropped them into the bowl. Then he poured the honey into the bowl and mixed the hair and honey together. The curls hissed and fizzed as they mixed with the honey. They waited for Sara and Emily to return with the babies' tears.

While they waited for the tears, the dragon went into the chasm to talk with Zoe and George. "I am sorry this happened. The fairies meant no harm."

"We know that, Mr. Dragon. I just wish they had waited to see what happened to the leprechaun. It was really amazing to see that bubble burst. The explosion was so loud. But that is all over now. What are we going to do?"

"Your mother remembered a spell in one of my books. We are preparing the potion now and will come here in a few minutes to do the spell. You and George need to find flowers that look like cups so that you can drink the potion. You will stand in the middle of this rock and we will sit in a circle around you. We will hold hands and chant the spell while you drink as much of the potion as possible. You cannot go outside of the circle. That is really important. Don't leave the circle.

"I must tell you that I know the spell will change you back into children, but I don't know what else it will do to you. When we have finished the spell you will need to be very honest with me. If you feel anything or sense anything that may be different I will need to help you. Do you understand?"

"What do you mean, Mr. Dragon? What else could happen to us?"

"I don't know. Sometimes spells make you a different color or they make you really big or really small. You will be George and Zoe, but you might not look exactly the same."

Zoe spoke for them both. "Mr. Dragon, we understand. We are glad to be rid of the leprechaun and if we must suffer some other consequence, then that is the way it is. We just want to be back to ourselves, not little fairies stuck in a chasm. We're ready."

The dragon smiled at them. "You know, you two are kind of cute in your little fairy outfits with the wings. I don't suppose…"

George yelled as loudly as his little fairy voice would allow, "No way, Mr. Dragon! I want to be a normal boy again without these wings and this weird outfit. How can the boy fairies even wear this green suit and have these pointy ears?"

They all laughed. "You are very brave. We will do everything we can. Wait here and we'll be back shortly."

The dragon left to find Sara and complete the potion. Zoe and George flew to the nearby bushes and found some flowers that could be used as cups. They sat on the flat rock to wait.

"George, what do you think is going to happen to us?"

"I'm not sure, Zoe. But I want you to know that you are the best sister that anyone could ever ask for and I love you."

"And you are the best and bravest brother anyone could ever hope for, George, even if you do have pointy ears. I think we will be fine."

Come Back to Me

Everyone came to the clearing. The dragon placed the pot with the honey and hair on the flat rock. Sara handed him the cup of tears. No one asked how Sara and Emily got the babies to cry, but they had collected plenty of tear drops. The dragon poured the tears into the pot and stirred the potion with his magic claw. He saw some smoke and some popping in the honey.

The adults sat in a circle around the flat rock. They held hands. Sara and Jim held one of the twin's hands and Emily and Katie held the other twin's hands so that they were included in the circle. The dragon stood behind the circle and explained the spell.

"Zoe and George must drink as much of the potion in the pot as they can. While they are drinking, everyone in the circle must chant, 'Come back to me'. Since I have never seen this spell in action I have no idea what will happen. It is very important that Zoe and George stay inside the circle and the adults cannot break the circle. Hold onto each other tightly. Is everyone ready?"

The adults nodded their heads. Zoe and George squeaked as loudly as they could, "Ready!"

The adults began to chant and Zoe and George took their flower cups and began to drink the potion. Even though it was made from honey, it really didn't taste very good. In fact, it tasted awful and it was so bubbly that the children started burping. But they kept drinking their flower cups of the potion until they couldn't sip another drop. They fell down on the rock exhausted and full.

The dragon walked around the outside of the circle encouraging the adults to keep saying the chant. "It is going to work. It just needs time." The adults kept saying over and over, "Come back to me." Everyone was getting tired and they were afraid the potion wasn't working. The adults began to look at each other with concern and doubt.

Suddenly there was a bright flash of light on the rock and then a big cloud of pink smoke rose up. The adults could no longer see Zoe and George in all the smoke, but they could hear the children coughing.

As the smoke blew away, there were Zoe and George standing on the rock with their eyes closed, holding hands. They looked like statues, they were so still.

"Zoe? George?" Sara called out.

The children opened their eyes, both said "Yuck!", and they stepped away from each other. "What am I doing holding my sister's hands?"

"It's not like I wanted to hold YOUR hands!"

And then they hugged each other. They were back, they were children, they were Zoe and George. They were still in those weird fairy costumes, Zoe's blue dress and George's green suit. They turned to the adults.

Everyone jumped up at once and began hugging them. There were shouts of joy and such celebration. "This will be a special Thanksgiving this year. Welcome back."

Then the dragon stepped forward. "Excuse me, everyone. I need a moment to check the children to see if they are all right." The dragon asked George and Zoe several questions to test their memory and how they were feeling. Everything checked out just fine. Both children said they felt some tingling on their fingertips and on their shoulders where the wings had been.

"I think the spell has worked," announced the dragon. The whole crowd left the chasm and headed for Matt and Katie's house.

* * * * * *

After a very happy celebratory dinner at Katie's, the families headed home. Tomorrow would be another family get-together and they had so much to be thankful for. Zoe and George stayed close together throughout the dinner and they held hands all the way home in the van. "Thanks, George, for always being there."

"Thanks for being the big sister. You always know what to do. That was brilliant how you tricked that leprechaun. Those gold coins sure worked. I'm glad we went to New York City to find them."

When they arrived home, everyone was ready to go to bed. Sara and Jim came in to wish their older children a good night. "I am so proud of you two. You were so brave and clever to trick that leprechaun. Good job!"

"And I finally got to see the dragon. All these years and all these stories. I just needed to open my eyes and believe," Dad said. "Sleep tight you two." They tucked George and Zoe into their beds and turned off the light. They left the door open a crack so the children could see the night light in the hallway. Sara and Jim checked on the twins and then headed to their own bedroom. The door clicked shut.

George turned on his flashlight and took a deep breath, "All right, Zoe, tell me what you are feeling right now."

"What do you mean, George?"

"Okay, I'll go first. My fingers are tingling and I feel like I could point them at an object and something would happen. But I don't know what and I am scared that I might break it or hurt it."

Zoe sat up in bed. "And my shoulders keep tingling like I feel that I could still fly without the wings. Isn't that weird?"

"Me, too. Let's try something."

George got out of bed and closed their bedroom door. Then he turned on the light. He found an old juice box in the trashcan and put it in the middle of their table near the window. "Let's see what happens." George pointed all ten of his fingers at the juice box and it began to float up into the air. He pointed to the wall and the box floated to the wall. He pointed back to the window and the box floated to the window.

"Did you see that? Did you see that?"

Zoe pointed at one of her dolls sitting in the corner. It floated up into the air. Zoe brought her hands towards herself and the doll floated over to Zoe in the bed. "Whoa! Is that cool or what?"

"So we can move things with our hands. Why are our shoulders tingling?"

Zoe stood up on her bed and jumped as high as she could towards the window. Instead of crashing to the floor, she floated ever so gracefully up to the ceiling. George jumped and he began to fly slowly around the bedroom. The two were giggling and laughing and so involved in their flying tricks that they did not realize that their parents were coming down the hallway.

The door swung open. "What is going on in here? You're going to wake the... Huh?" Sara and Jim stood in the doorway and watched Zoe and George fly around their bedroom. The children landed near their parents and said, "Watch this!"

They both pointed at stuffed animals on the shelf and they began to float around the room. As the children pointed this way and that, the animals floated to their commands.

"Oh my. The dragon said this might happen. You need to rest tonight and tomorrow we are going to talk with him about this. And you need to be careful. If these powers suddenly disappear and you are way up in the sky, or if you are trying to move something and it crashes, it could be disastrous. Just don't do anything drastic or foolish. We need to understand what has happened. Time to get some sleep."

The children floated down to their beds and pointed the animals back to the shelves. Sara and Jim tucked the children back into bed. "Now you need to rest. Tomorrow will be a very busy day and you will need all of your energy. And be very careful with these powers. They may not last. Sleep."

"Okay, we get the message."

The door was left ajar and they could hear their parents going down the hallway. Then their door clicked shut again. "George, what else should we do?"

"Well, don't you wonder about the twins? Do you think anything happened to Annie and Nate? Don't you think we should check them out?"

The two tiptoed out of bed and crept into the babies' room. They could hear the two babies singing to each other in their soft baby voices. George peeked over the top of the crib and saw Annie pointing her fingers at the mobile that hung over their bed. As she moved her hand, the mobile spun around. When she stopped, the mobile froze. George's eyes grew big and he turned to Zoe.

"Look at Annie! She is moving the mobile."

"What? That can't be." Zoe peaked over the top of the crib and stared at the twins. They were both pointing at the mobile and making it spin. Then the twins held hands and together they slowly floated up to Zoe's eye level. They giggled and waved to Zoe.

Zoe whispered to the twins, "You two need to go to sleep now. Drift down to the bed and go night-night." The twins smiled and slowly drifted down to the mattress. They closed their eyes and went to sleep. Zoe quietly slid down to the floor. She motioned to George to follow her out the door. They crawled back to their room.

As Zoe closed the door, she whispered to George, "What are we going to do? Babies can't float around like that. They can't have powers like that. They won't know how to control them. Things could get out of hand."

"Zoe, I think Mom and Dad are right. We need to sleep and get ready for tomorrow. We'll see if all four of us still have these powers in the morning. The dragon should know what to do. We're not going to solve this tonight, so let's get some sleep. Goodnight, Zoe. I love you, big sis."

"You're right, George. Tomorrow will be soon enough for our family to figure out what to do. Goodnight, big brother."

The children drifted off to sleep wondering what these new magical powers were all about. Hopefully the dragon would have some answers in the morning. And that will be a tale for another day.

Made in the USA
Charleston, SC
30 May 2016